Freak   e

By

Katie Lee O'Guinn

Book 1 in the Lost Witch Trilogy

To my beloved little Chitlins, You bring me joy, purpose and love. This book is for you.

Books By Katie Lee O'Guinn

Freak of Nature

Blood Rush

Fate Changer

Werewolf Dreams

Werewolf Rage

Werewolf Revenge

Contents

Chapter 1- Priorities

"For the millionth time, I'm not a witch," Sarah said as calmly and rationally as she humanly could.

Lena Hudson stared unbelievingly at her niece and rolled her eyes. She was a short, curvy woman, with a long almost beaky nose.

"You're a witch. Just saying you're not doesn't make it true. Honestly Sarah, you'd think you'd be excited about it," Lena said.

"If you want to see me excited, invite Billie Joe Armstrong to dinner," she said and blew a wayward lock of red hair out of her eyes. She glanced behind her at the door and inched closer hoping she could actually get through it before this conversation escalated into all-out war.

"Like the lead singer of Green Day would come anywhere near Huntingdon Pennsylvania or you for that matter. Forget your crappy music and listen to me. You're eighteen years old now Sarah, stop acting like a child and come tonight. We can teach you how to make your power stronger," Lena said, her pale brown eyebrows coming down into a harsh V. She ran her hands anxiously through her short cap of mousy brown hair and looked almost scared for a moment.

Sarah huffed out a breath and grabbed her backpack, slipping it on her shoulder and opening the door as quickly as she could. She didn't have time for this.

"Thanks, but no thanks. I've done the research, Lena. I have psychokinesis with a few other talents thrown in. It's actually very normal. Most people have some form of it just to a lesser degree. Google it."

Lena hissed out a breath and started to look seriously mad. "I think I know a little more about you than Google. You're being childish and I've just about lost my patience with you."

Sarah walked out the door and lifted a hand in a carefree wave. Having the same conversation with Lena over and over was a pain, but it was better than the alternative. Actually going to her aunt's freak show she called a *meeting*. *As if*. Three emotionally disturbed women, one creeper guy that gave her the willies every single time she saw him and her dear old aunt. No thank you. She was already weird enough as it was. She didn't need to label herself a witch. She could just imagine what the food tasted like in the State Mental ward. *Gag.*

Sarah walked the three blocks to Huntingdon High. She passed the shop windows and glanced at her reflection with a slight frown. She looked pretty much the same as always. She might have grown a little taller over the summer and since she'd started running, she'd gone from average, to thin and toned. Her long wavy red hair still fell in waves around her face and down her back and her green eyes were still staring back at her the same way they always had. Bleak, tired and expectant. What she was waiting for she didn't know yet.

She couldn't wait for this year to be over. Just one more year with her aunt and she'd be gone the day after graduation. Living with the constant pressure from her aunt to join in her strange activities was wearing on her. When she had been a kid, Lena had been different. Almost manically energetic and fun as if she were trying to prove to everyone that she could take care of Sarah better than anyone else. When she realized that no one really cared one way or another, she relaxed into who she really was: A woman who had custody of her niece but spent the majority of her time and money on herself and her own pursuits, leaving Sarah to her own devices most of the time.

Sarah hadn't minded. She didn't enjoy Lena's company that much and spent most of her time engrossed in books. Friends came and went in elementary school, but when Sarah reached Jr. High she changed and everyone stayed far, far away from her. She had made her peace with being an outcast but she couldn't say she enjoyed it.

It was the first day of her senior year and she was not excited about it. She quickly passed groups of kids walking in packs. Some people called out hello, but most of them ignored her, *or pretended to*. It wasn't easy to ignore Sarah Hudson. Her large green eyes, pale freckled skin and serious smile made people stare, but it was more than that. It was as if people couldn't help but stare. Sarah had grown used to it. She ignored it mainly, because when someone got curious and came closer they usually wished they hadn't.

Sarah sang the lyrics to Green Day's song, *I Walk Alone*, softly as she passed the last group of teenagers and tried to ignore the blatant stares of a few jocks. The faint sound of a wolf whistle made her grind her teeth in irritation. *Idiot*. He might be brave enough to whistle but there was no way he'd actually engage her in conversation. What a wimp.

She shook off the sudden blast of emptiness and tried for a little tolerance. She knew why they didn't, *couldn't* come up to her. What kept people back at a safe distance was the invisible force of energy that she was unable to ditch. When people approached her, it was almost as if they were hit by a large dose of static electricity. Her teachers at school were the best at dealing with it. If people would just give it ten or fifteen minutes, they got used to the feeling and were able to ignore it. Most people weren't patient though. Her science partner from last year, Jill Cavanaugh had gotten so used to her that she barely winced when she sat down next to her. That didn't mean that she had ever once been invited to Jill's pool parties though. Luckily for her, no one had tried to analyze her. She accepted her fate as an outcast and people left her alone. The alternative was being recognized as what she really was. *A freak of nature.*

Sarah put her back pack in her locker and headed for first period, English. Her English classes were always her favorite and she knew she was lucky to have gotten Mr. Terrence. She'd had him last year for Creative Writing. He was a large black man with a booming laugh and a gift for poetry. Unlike everyone else, he always smiled at her and if he noticed her strange energy he never held it against her.

She sat down in a seat in the front row and immediately tried to drown out the back ground noise of students and the announcements coming across the intercom. She took a piece of gum out of her purse and flipped her hair over her shoulder but stopped when she felt a warm breeze slide down her head and back as if someone had reached out and touched her. No, *caressed* her. Sarah shivered and slowly turned around and found her eyes locked with a boy she'd never seen before. He looked tall and strong, like an athlete. His wavy dark blond hair had to have been professionally styled and his eyes glinted silver at her. His high cheek bones and strong jaw line would have all the girls drooling within seconds. He looked solemnly back at her, not flinching and not looking away. Just looking at her as if he had every right to.

Sarah swallowed and turned slowly back to the front of the class. And then she felt it again. That slow warm breeze, moving from the top of her head down her back, but this time it wrapped around her and moved to her mouth as if it were a kiss. She shivered uncontrollably again and licked her lips. This was no coincidence. Something was going on. She closed her eyes and tried to use the energy she carried around with her as a shield to move out from her body and move it towards the back of the room and the new boy. She had to know if he was the one touching her.

"I'm Zane Miner. You must be Sarah Hudson."

Sarah opened her eyes and whipped her head up to see the new boy standing directly beside her. This was just weird. Boys hadn't come up to her voluntarily since before she had turned thirteen. They sure liked to stare at her, but actually engaging her in conversation without stuttering and tripping over themselves was a rarity. Sarah stared up into Zane's direct, clear gray eyes and smiled as she felt the warm breeze wrap around her again.

"And how would you know what my name is?" she asked with a raised eyebrow and a polite smile.

Zane snagged the desk behind him and pulled it closer to hers, sitting down and leaning closer.

"I asked."

Sarah swallowed and bit her lip. *Holy crap.* This guy was actually talking to her, possibly flirting with her and best of all, not wincing and falling over himself to get away from her. This was *not* normal.

"Hmmm. So did you just move into town?" she asked, keeping her eye out for Mr. Terence. She sighed in relief as he strode into the classroom. Thank heavens. He would start class and she could have forty-five minutes to re-group and figure out this new guy. But just as Mr. Terrence was about to open his mouth, Zane turned his head and stared hard at the teacher. All of a sudden, his books and papers fell out of his arms, making a huge mess. A few kids jumped up to help Mr. Terrence as a cloud of what possibly sounded like profanity floated softly through the air. Sarah turned back to Zane, looking at him suspiciously.

Zane grinned and scooted even closer to her seat. "Yeah, I'm new in town. My mom and I moved in with my grandma just this last weekend. She was diagnosed with Alzheimer's so we'll be around for a while."

Sarah forgot Mr. Terrence and focused completely on Zane. "You wouldn't happen to be Agnes Adam's grandson would you? I was so sad when they closed the book store. It's my favorite place in town."

Zane smiled and nodded. "The Noble Barn was my grandma's pride and joy. My mom's opening it back up today."

Sarah smiled in pleasure. The Noble Barn had been a haven for her for the last few years since her aunt had gone loony. Her smile turned to a frown though when she felt Zane slide his foot across the floor and touch hers. Sarah immediately felt a warmth slide up her leg. She closed her eyes as she concentrated on the feeling and used her senses to follow the feeling back to its source. She felt the warmth go back down her leg and through her foot and into Zane. Her eyes flew open and locked with Zane's as she followed the path and felt a part of her energy move up the boy and wrap around his torso. She swallowed as she realized Zane was grinning at her.

"Well that settles it. What are you doing after school?"

9

Sarah felt herself blush and slid her foot away from Zane's. "Um, I've got the usual. Homework, chores and stuff."

Zane shook his head and reached over and touched his finger to the back of her hand. A small spark erupted from the contact and she gasped and jerked her hand away, staring at him.

Zane leaned back away from her and took out his pen and notebook. "Forget your stuff. Let's hang out."

Sarah raised her eyebrows and shook her head slowly. "I don't even know you."

Zane shook his head and smiled. "You mean you don't know me *yet*."

Sarah swallowed nervously and looked away. *Who was this guy?* He not only ignored her electrical fence he seemed drawn to it.

Sarah had never been so relieved when Mr. Terrence threw the pile of papers on his desk and glared at the classroom. "Open your laptops and let's get started on Beowulf."

A half an hour later and with ten minutes left of class, Sarah glanced down at where Zane had touched her hand and noticed a mark that hadn't been there before. Almost like a smudge from a pen or something. She licked her finger and rubbed at the spot but it didn't fade. She brought her hand closer to her face and stared at the mark. It was a very small bird. She brought her hand closer to her face and squinted. The detail was so precise she could see the individual feathers. *No. Way.* She lowered her hand to the desk and turned her head slowly to look at the boy she had done her very best to ignore for the last half hour. He was staring right at her, not smiling and not frowning, just looking at her as if he could read her mind. *Or like he was trying to.*

She stared back for a moment and then raised her hand. She wasn't ready for this. She had to process this last half hour before she was pressured into hanging out with a guy who could tattoo her hand just by touching her. This was getting too crazy even for her.

"Yes Sarah?" Mr. Terence asked.

"May I be excused from class early? I'm not feeling well."

Mr. Terrence looked at her doubtfully but waved his hand in acquiescence.

"Um Mr. Terrence? Can Sarah show me to my next class on her way to the office? I'm not sure where it is and it's my first day here," Zane said.

Mr. Terrence smiled kindly at Zane and looked sharply at Sarah. "Excellent idea. Off you go."

Sarah groaned quietly as she put her laptop away and grabbed her purse. As she reached the door, Zane put his hand on the small of her back, giving a slight but not unpleasant shock. He opened the door for her and then continued down the hallway with her. His hand remaining on her back in either a protective manner or a proprietary manner, she couldn't tell which.

"You're touching me. People don't touch me," Sarah muttered with a dark frown.

Zane looked down at her from his 6 foot height and shrugged. "I'm not like other people. But let me know if I do something that makes you uncomfortable."

Sarah shook her head in confusion. "Everything about you makes me uncomfortable. *Who are you?* I mean, most people can't come within 3 feet of me and you're acting like a magnet. And you marked me! Like, is this permanent? Seriously, who are you?" Sarah demanded, stopping in the middle of the empty hallway.

Zane stopped too, his hand falling away from her back as he turned to face her. Sarah stared up at him, breathing fast with her heart racing. He stepped closer to her and cupped his hands around her face. She immediately felt that strange pleasant warmth seep into her skin and she stepped closer before she knew what she was doing. He smiled and tilted her face up towards him.

"I recognized you were different as soon as you stepped onto the grounds of the school. I could feel you coming closer as you were walking down the street. I can feel the blood coursing through your veins and through your heart. I'm like you."

Sarah blinked quickly and tried to step back, putting her hand on Zane's chest. "What do you mean *like* me? What do you think I am?" she asked, her voice shaking.

Zane placed his hand over the top of hers on his chest and closed his eyes as she felt some of her energy leave and enter him.

"You're a witch of course, just like me."

Sarah's mouth opened in shock as she jerked her hand out of Zane's grasp. "*No*," she said, shaking her head firmly. "I have psychokinesis but I'm not a witch. There's a book about people just like me. You can buy it on Amazon. *No*. There's no way I'm a witch. That's crazy," she whispered.

Zane looked genuinely surprised. "You pushed my power back with your foot! You have an energy field bigger and brighter than anyone's I've ever seen. You can call it psychokinesis if you want, but from where I'm standing, you're a witch."

Sarah felt something that could have been tears mist her eyes as she pulled back from Zane shaking her head. "I don't have to be anything I don't want to be."

Zane's mouth twitched up on one side as he studied her with compassion. "That's like a wolf saying he's just a little puppy. We really need to hang out. There are a few things we need to talk about. First priority would have to be you accepting yourself."

Sarah continued to inch away from Zane. "And what's the second priority?"

Zane grinned at her. "Me of course. Although if you want to make me first, I'm okay with that too."

Chapter 2 - Porch Lights

Sarah peeked out of the bathroom, scanning the hallway for Zane. Fourth period had just ended and Zane had popped up three more times since English. Of course the last two times he had been surrounded by groups of girls flipping their hair and flirting like crazy. She had walked past him, trying as hard as she could to ignore him, but he'd still managed to reach out between a cheerleader and the captain of the softball team and touched her arm. The girls had all turned around and when they saw who he was talking to, stared in shock when he had called out, *'See you at lunch, Sarah.'*

Sarah shook her head in amazement at his cockiness and huffed out an impatient breath. Sure he was gorgeous. Yes he could stand her company and seemed determined to stay in it. But going from zero to sixty was not her style and she was not going to be pushed into anything until she was good and ready. Especially with a guy who not only thought she was a witch, but thought he was a witch too.

She pushed through the cafeteria doors and automatically scanned for Lash. Lash was the only reason she inflicted the cafeteria on herself. One large room filled with clique after clique after clique. And none of them seemed receptive to including her for some strange reason. She'd much rather be in a quiet little cubicle in the library but saving Lash from the ever-present bullies won every time. For some reason, she just couldn't ignore him or his sad eyes.

She remembered the first time she'd seen Lash. He and his father had moved into town when she was in the third grade. He'd been a skinny, pale weak little thing and had been easy game for the school yard predators. Not much had changed since then. She grinned as she remembered the feeling of breaking Jackson Hathaway's nose after she'd found him holding Lash's head in the toilet. *Good times.*

She caught a glance of jet black hair and made her way to the lunch line, standing two people behind Lash. She didn't break people's noses anymore. She'd found better ways to stick up for Lash. Anyone who bumped into Lash, making him drop his lunch found that their pants magically fell to their ankles. Last month when Rod Carey, a two hundred pound jerk, decided to show off in front of Charity Klein, he found that the hamburger he'd snagged off Lash's tray and crammed down his throat was determined to come right back up. All of the kids still teased Rod about his queasy stomach.

She glanced around the room trying to scan for danger when the conversation in front of her started to sink in.

"Lash, you have the most gorgeous blue eyes."

Sarah's eyes widened as she turned to see who in their right mind was coming on to Lash. Her mouth fell open when she realized it was Jill Cavanaugh. Jill was gorgeous, rich, smart and one of the nicest girls at school. *What the heck?* She inched closer and glanced at Lash. Lash grinned at Jill and then noticed Sarah staring.

"Hey Sarah, how's it going?" Lash asked with a twinkle in his eye.

Sarah smiled back and gave him the thumbs up signal behind Jill's back. "Great Lash. Life is great."

"Lash, there you are *you freak*."

Sarah frowned, her eyes turning to slits as she moved quickly in front of Lash and Jill. Rod was back, wanting someone to pick on. His hulking frame came within inches of her. He barely winced as he came up against her energy. He was too focused on Lash.

"Rod, the end of the line is back there. Take off," she said in a steely voice, glaring at him and trying to think of something to do that wouldn't look suspicious and bring unwanted attention on her.

"You're always sticking up for Lash," Rod said. "It kind of makes me wonder. You in love with this wimp? You think you're such a big man, right Lash? You need a girl to fight your battles for you?"

Sarah felt Lash move around her and she groaned hoping he didn't bleed too much before she could come up with some way to stop it. She glanced over and then surprised herself by having to look up. Lash must have grown a little over the summer. *Or a lot.* Of course she hadn't seen him in three months since he had spent the summer in Harrisburg with his dad. This was the first time she'd had to look up to see his face. She glanced at his ripped arms and her eyebrows rose in surprise as she looked closer at Lash. He looked good. His black hair was longer than most guys' hair but it went well with his cheek bones. His face looked more hardened, more sculpted than last year. He looked like a man now. Holy crap. *Lash was hot.*

She stepped back and watched what Lash would do, prepared to have Rod's pants fall to his ankles the second he looked like he was going to start swinging.

"Rod, I'd be happy to kick your butt here and now, but I don't want to get expelled and I know you don't want to get expelled. So just cool off and get out of here."

Rod glanced around and noticed that two teachers were already looking at him suspiciously. He shrugged and sneered at Lash. "I've got unfinished business with you Lash. Don't forget it."

Lash sneered back as Rod walked away. Sarah grinned as Rod's pants fell quietly in a rush of denim to his ankles showing his bright blue plaid boxers to a large group of sophomore girls. The cacophony of giggles and Rod's bright red face had her laughing to herself as she turned back to the lunch line.

Lash's hand on her shoulder had her looking up. "You didn't have to do that. I mean, . . . you don't have to do that *anymore*," he said quietly, leaning down so no one else could hear.

Sarah blushed as she stared up into Lash's bright blue eyes. "I don't know what you mean."

Lash grinned at her and touched her cheek. "You've been sticking up for me since the 3rd grade Sarah. Maybe it's time I started looking out for you instead," he said with a half grin that had her staring.

Jill cleared her throat loudly and touched Lash's arm. "Lash, let's go sit in the corner so we can talk, okay?"

Lash looked down at Sarah for an extra second and then followed Jill. Sarah laughed softly to herself and picked up her tray. It was a good day when Lash stuck up for himself and looked good doing it.

She usually sat at the table with the best visual of Lash and known bullies. She'd pretend to read a book, ignoring the groups of kids around her, or even occasionally joining in a conversation after the kids got used to her energy. Now what was she supposed to do?

"I saved you a seat Sarah. Come on, I've been waiting for you," Zane said, appearing in front of her. He took her tray out of her hands forcing her to follow him.

He walked past the hopeful stares of the most beautiful girls in school and picked a table for two in the very back of the lunch room.

She sat down opposite Zane and glanced around noticing that half the lunch room was staring at them. Lash and Jill were at a table two rows away and Lash was staring at Zane in a dark way that made her look twice. There were some strange undercurrents floating around.

"I guess we're the newest exhibit at the zoo today," she said, wishing she didn't blush so easily.

Zane shrugged and opened his chocolate milk. "For you and me, people are always going to stare. They can't help it. They don't even know why they're staring. They can't figure it out. What is it about Sarah Hudson that draws people's eyes?"

Sarah glanced at the table of girls staring at Zane, just begging him to look back and grinned. "Whatever. I do believe I'll use my witch mind-reading skills. *Hmmm,* yes, got it. Why is that gorgeous guy sitting with *her* when he should be sitting with *me?*" she said in a high pitched annoying Barbie voice.

Zane laughed and glanced at the table of girls still staring at him. He winked and waved at the girls but then turned his whole attention back to Sarah.

"They're like moth's drawn to a porch light. Unfortunately, porch lights aren't drawn to moths."

Sarah looked down at her chicken nuggets and corn and tried not to smile. She pushed the tray away and leaned her chin on her hands.

"So you're a porch light huh?"

Zane grabbed her chicken nuggets and gave her an apple from his back pack. She took it gratefully and rubbed it on her shirt.

"Right now, I'm the moth to your light," he said with a sweet smile that had her heart jumping.

Sarah shook her head laughing. "That was such a line."

Zane smiled and grabbed her hand. Sarah immediately felt the warmth seep into her cool hand and flood her body. She breathed in deeply and felt her face flush, not from embarrassment, but from warmth. She looked down at the bird he had marked her hand with and watched it fade quickly until it was as if it had never been there. She pulled her hand slowly out of Zane's grasp and looked away.

Zane leaned back and shook his head, glancing around the lunch room. "So walk me through this. I couldn't help overhearing that guy over there, who's still staring at you by the way. What's your history with him? Why are you sticking up for him?"

Sarah looked over at Lash, surprised to find that he was still looking at her and Zane. He didn't look happy. She looked away in confusion.

"Um, I don't know. Poor little kid moves to town when he's eight and every jerk in a four mile radius wants to pound him into dust. I step in occasionally. End of story."

Zane looked over his shoulder at Lash until Lash finally looked away. Zane shook his head and took another chicken nugget. "That guy's no poor little kid now. He's got a really strange aura too. Do you see that dark brown, greenish light he's emitting? That's not normal and it's definitely not good."

Sarah leaned forward and looked at Lash who was now in deep conversation with Jill. She tried to see some color around Lash but all she could see were shoulders where before he'd been so tiny and skinny. Holy cow, what had happened to Lash? *Steroids*? How blind could she have been to miss shoulders like that?

"I don't see anything Zane."

Zane shrugged and put the cap back on his milk. "Regardless of his aura, weird as it is, that guy can fight his own battles now. Using your skills to rip that guy's pants off was hilarious, but unnecessary from where I'm sitting."

Sarah grinned. "Humiliating bullies is how I get my cheap thrills."

Zane's gray eyes brightened immediately as he leaned over the table towards her. "Thrill seeker, huh?"

Sarah swallowed nervously and put the apple down. She'd never had a boyfriend before, she'd never even been kissed and this guy was too much for her to handle. She was smart enough to know that.

"Look Zane, like I said, you're gorgeous and you're intriguing and you understand things about me that I don't even understand myself. But you're coming on too strong. I'm embarrassed to admit this, but I don't know the first thing about how to handle you. You intimidate me. You make me nervous. You look at me differently. You see me and I'm not used to people seeing me."

"You mean you're not used to someone looking at you, seeing the real you, liking what they see and wanting to get to know you better?" Zane said, sounding serious.

Sarah pushed her hair behind her ear and leaned back in her chair, folding her arms across her chest. "Yeah. I mean, I don't know what to do with you. You're completely out of my realm of experience. And you say you want to hang out. What exactly does that entail?"

Zane turned his head and smiled, causing a girl at the nearest table to drop her Doritos bag on the floor.

"Well, being a porch light, I have to admit I don't have a lot of experience with moths or even other porch lights since there are so few porch lights my age that are stunning, like you for instance. I think you're making a bigger deal out of this than it is. It's just a boy, who happens to be a witch, meeting a beautiful female witch and wanting to do a happy dance. What you see as coming on strong is just me expressing my happiness, glee and joy."

Sarah tilted her head and studied Zane. Was he a player or was he just a witch excited about finding another witch? *Oops, someone with telekinesis.* "Your happiness, joy and glee are a little over-powering."

Zane winced and looked away, but then sat up straight and leaned towards her. "Sarah, when I felt you walking towards me and then I saw you, this gorgeous red head, emitting enough energy to light up the East coast, I couldn't contain myself. I apologize for coming on too strong so I've got a deal for you. I'll slow down; I'll back off a little if you'll agree to be friends," he said, holding out his hand for a shake.

Sarah looked at his hand suspiciously until he lowered it. "*Just* friends? Like you're in the friend zone kind of friend?"

Zane laughed and shook his head, grinning at her. "Now you're talking crazy. Nah, just friends until you're a little more comfortable with me. There will be no friend zone with you and me. This is called a waiting period."

Sarah groaned and ran her fingers through her hair. "Waiting for what exactly?"

Zane leaned back in his chair and looked directly into her eyes, like no other person ever had before and stopped smiling. "I'm comfortable with the term boyfriend."

Sarah's mouth fell open and she clenched her hands on her knees. "That's what I'm talking about Zane. We just met in first period. It's only lunch time. I'm scared by the end of the day we're going to be married with two kids. You have got to stop freaking me out. You are in the friend zone as of right this second. Friend zone or I'm putting a restraining order on you. Deal?" she said, holding her hand out.

Zane grabbed her hand quickly and smiled as the energy flowed between them, making Sarah's hair curl and her eyes turn bright.

"You're breaking my heart, but friend zone it is. If you ever want me to come out of that particular zone, you only have to say the word. Until then, you are my very special friend. Do I get to flirt with you? Friends do flirt you know."

Sarah pulled her hand away and grinned. "Just on Fridays."

Zane groaned and gathered their garbage up. Sarah stood up and glanced around, automatically trying to find Lash. She frowned as she saw Lash and Jill slip out the side door that led out into the parking lot. *Where were those two going?* She forgot about Lash though as Zane's warm breeze wrapped around her torso and squeezed her.

She glared at Zane and punched him in the arm. "You're going to have to teach me how to do that."

Zane slung a friendly arm around her shoulders as they walked towards the lockers. "That my *friend* is why we need to hang out. It's time, my little witch that you learn to do more than strip unsuspecting jocks of their clothes."

Sarah giggled as she pushed Zane's arm off her shoulders. "Nothing dark and creepy though. I hate that heavy gross feeling I get when I'm around people who practice witchy stuff."

Zane looked at her in confusion. *"Dark and creepy?* Do I look like a creeper to you? Do I feel dark or heavy?" he asked tilting her chin up.

Sarah shook her head and looked down feeling bad for some reason. "No, you feel good. When I'm around you I just feel warm . . . and strange. Well, not strange, but just um . . . I don't know, *happy?"*

Zane tilted his head and looked torn for a moment. "You sure you want me in the friend zone? Because that calls for a kiss."

Sarah laughed nervously and pushed him away. "Stop flirting, it's only Monday."

Zane groaned loudly and pulled her toward his locker, where without twirling the lock, he just touched the metal and it swung open. Sarah glanced around nervously, hoping no one saw.

"So who have you been around that gives you that dark, heavy icky feeling, just out of curiosity? Let me guess, Lash."

Sarah leaned against a locker and looked away, ignoring the stares of the kids walking past her. "My aunt and her freak show friends," she said quietly, looking down at her shoes.

Zane shut the locker and leaned his shoulder on the locker next to her. "I would never make you feel that way Sarah. Hang out with me after school. Come meet my mom. She can tell you everything you need to know about being a witch. She's taught me everything I know."

Sarah sighed and looked up into Zane's soft gray eyes. He looked sincere, but more than that, he looked kind. Besides, it was that or go home and face her aunt and her weekly *meeting*.

"Okay."

Zane held up his finger when his phone vibrated. She watched him read his text but then looked around at the kids, wondering what normal people did after school. She glanced down the hallway and was surprised to see Lash push through the front doors with Jill Cavanaugh's hand in his. Her eyebrows rose in surprise. *Lash holding hands with a girl.* And he really did look different. Gone was the pasty white skin from last year. He was practically glowing with healthy color. His eyes were bright and wide and he looked like he was practically pulsing with strength and life. He held his head differently now too. Where before he had always let his head hang down, not wanting to be noticed, his head was up and he grinned almost triumphantly as he made his way down the hallway. The same girls who stared at Zane, were now staring at Lash in almost the same way. He had a dark magnetism that she'd never noticed before but she was sure feeling it now.

Sarah tore her eyes away from Lash and finally noticed Jill. Jill looked happy, but kind of ill too. Her skin looked pale and there was sweat on her forehead as if she'd just run the mile. She stumbled a little but Lash grabbed her arm, steadying her. She smiled dreamily up into his face and kept walking. Lash grinned back down at her. He noticed Sarah staring at him and he looked surprised and almost guilty. He looked down for a moment and then back at Sarah with a shrug. He left Jill at her locker and then walked up to her.

"I would never be with Jill if I knew I could be with you Sarah," he said, leaning in so he was practically touching her ear. "I'm good enough for you now. I'm strong enough for you now. Just say the word Sarah," he said, pulling back.

Sarah glanced at Zane whose face had turned hard and mean as he stood close enough to hear. He put his phone back in his pocket and stood up straighter, crossing his arms across his chest.

Sarah cleared her throat and looked back at Lash. "Lash, I didn't know you felt that way about me."

Lash glanced over his shoulder at Jill who was content to wait for him at her locker. "I'll give you some time to think about it," he said in a strangely purposeful way and then walked back to Jill.

Sarah shivered, feeling cold and sad all of a sudden.

"Man, if that guy's aura gets any darker it's going to be black as tar," Zane said, staring coldly at the back of Lash's head.

"He's had a rough time Zane. Don't judge him," she said, automatically sticking up for Lash.

Zane shook his head and pushed away from the locker as the bell rang for fifth period. "I don't think you should be around somebody that dark Sarah. I'm just pointing that out as a friend."

Sarah sighed and walked Zane to his next class since he didn't know where the PE room was. If Zane thought Lash was dark, what would he think of her aunt?

Chapter 3 - Meet the Parent

Sarah felt the rush of kids push past her as she walked slowly to her locker. It had been one of the strangest days of her life and she still couldn't wrap her mind around it. It had started out so typical too. Fight with aunt. *Check*. Walk to school. *Check*. But from first period on? Life had decided to throw her into the deep end and she was still struggling to catch her breath. Was she really contemplating spending the afternoon with a guy she had just met that morning? Sarah Hudson did not do things like that. *Ever*. And then Lash changing on her. He'd gone from a little geeky guy she had a soft spot for to a hot guy that had a soft spot for her. That was the strangest thing of all. Something was going on with him. She had no clue what, but she was going to find out.

"You like making men wait for you huh? So typically female Sarah. I was hoping you'd surprise me," Zane said, standing by her locker and tapping his watch.

Sarah shook her head and tried to look mean, but she couldn't help smiling. What wasn't to smile about? This tall, lean, strong and handsome guy was determined to hang out with her. It was Christmas morning and she was acting like Scrooge. Maybe it was time to start living a little.

"Well, I'm here now Zane. Let me put my books away and we can go," she said as he reached out and played with her hair.

Sarah touched her locker with her finger and used her energy to open the lock. It popped open and she smiled in satisfaction. Zane grinned at her and then looked at her locker through slitted eyes. The metal on the door looked like it was melting and drooping for a few seconds, but then it slowly returned to its original shape.

Sarah's eye's widened in surprise. Opening a locker was one thing. Melting metal? That was far beyond anything she could do. "Okay. *Wow*. Can you teach me how to do that?" she asked, shaking her head in awe.

Zane grabbed the books out of her arms and put them in the locker for her, slamming it shut and twirling the lock. "Well, it kind of all depends. Witches are like people, we're all different and we have different talents. I'm pretty good with metal, but you might not be. It'll be interesting to find out what you are good at though. You're definitely a pro at manipulating clothing."

Sarah laughed and walked through the school doors and into the parking lot. "So are we walking or riding a bus or do you have a car?" she asked looking at him questioningly.

Zane pointed towards the parking lot and put his hand on the small of her back as they walked past groups of kids laughing and talking. "It's the silver jeep on the last row," he said pointing to what looked like a brand new jeep.

Sarah stared at Zane feeling slightly uncomfortable. "Yikes, you're rich."

Zane rolled his eyes. "Don't be a snob Sarah. Money is a just a thing. It was a gift from my Aunt Julie. She's a computer tech genius and she likes to spoil us since she doesn't have kids of her own."

Sarah let Zane open the door for her and she hopped up into the plush leather seat. Zane joined her a few seconds later and they roared out of the parking lot. "So who is *us*?"

Zane handed her his phone. "Check out my screen saver."

Sarah drew her finger across the Android phone opening up to the screen saver and saw Zane surrounded by three beautiful blond women, standing on a beach in what looked like Hawaii.

"Your family?"

Zane grinned and nodded. "My two sisters, Cat and Zandra and my mom is in the back. Her name's Gretchen. You'll love them."

Sarah winced and nodded. People had a way of not loving her. But if they were anything like Zane then there was a possibility. "So are your sisters witches like you and me?" she asked hopefully.

Zane snorted and shook his head, laughing at the thought. "Cat? Nah, she's up at college studying business and Zandra works for a non-profit organization in New York to help free kids from slavery in other countries. They're cool, but not witches."

Sarah nodded her head and felt disappointed. It would have been so nice to have met some female witches like Zane. Nice, kind, open and friendly. Someone she could talk to about what it was like. Someone she could be friends with.

"So your mom? What exactly is she like? Is she like you?" she asked hopefully.

Zane laughed again and shook his head. "Nah, we're kind of polar opposites, but we love each other, so it's all good. Here we are. Come in and make up your mind for yourself," he said turning off the jeep and opening his door.

Zane had driven them to The Noble Barn, his grandmother's bookstore that had been closed for a couple months because of her illness. She stared up at the old red brick building on main street with the green awnings and brightly lit window filled with books and posters. It was her favorite place to go, but for some reason, she didn't feel like getting out of the jeep.

Now, just hours after meeting a new guy at school, she was meeting his mother. *Who was a witch.* Yeah, this was no big deal.

Zane opened her car door and looked at her quizzically. "Are you an old fashioned girl Sarah? You like your men to open doors for you?"

Sarah giggled weakly and hopped out. "I'm strong enough to push a door open. I just happen to be a little nervous about meeting your mom is all. No biggee."

Zane smiled and pulled her in for a hug. "Oh, that's sweet. Now stop being a wimp."

Sarah swallowed as Zane pulled her through the front doors of Agnes Adam's book store and café, The Noble Barn. She'd always loved wandering the aisles of the little book store. Everyone in town usually drove into Harrisburg to shop at the mall and the book stores there, but she preferred this one. It was so peaceful and calm. She always left the store feeling ten times better than when she'd arrived.

"I'm sorry about your grandmother by the way," she said quietly, reaching out to touch Zane's arm.

Zane reached over and put his hand on top of hers, filling them both with warmth. "Alzheimer's is no joke. My mom's hoping to pull her out of it, but witches are humans too."

Sarah's mouth fell open in shock. "Are you telling me your grandmother, Agnes Adams was, *is* a witch?" she demanded stopping in front of a table filled with children's books about dinosaurs.

Zane looked surprised. "You seriously didn't know? A witch can always tell another witch. I knew the second you walked through the door. *Huh,*" he said looking at her like she was defective.

Sarah sniffed and turned away. "I block out as much as I can of that stuff. But I will say that I always felt so good when I came here. And Agnes always gave me free cookies and told me the most interesting stories about Ireland where her parents were from. I always wished she was my grandma," she said softly.

Zane pulled her in for a hug and kissed the top of her head. "Release me from the friend zone and she's yours."

Sarah laughed and realized she was leaning her head on Zane's chest. "Knock it off Zane."

Zane laughed and turned around as if he was looking at someone. A tall, beautiful blond woman of about forty-five walked around a book shelf and came towards them, smiling warmly and holding out a hand to Zane.

"Zane, who is this gorgeous creature? Trust you to find the prettiest girl in town on your first day of school," she said coming closer and looking curiously at Sarah.

As she reached out a hand to shake Sarah's, she paused and looked like she felt a strong shock. Her smile wavered slightly, but then came back bigger and brighter.

"Oh, you're a strong one, aren't you? Well come in and have a treat on the house," she said turning around and waving towards the café counter.

Sarah winced and looked at Zane worriedly. Zane shook his head and smiled encouragingly. "Relax," he ordered and pulled her towards the muffins Gretchen was already putting on plates.

"Coffee, hot chocolate or tea?" Gretchen asked looking at her expectantly.

"Hot chocolate sounds good," Sarah said, trying to smile.

Gretchen poured their drinks and leaned on the counter as she and Zane started eating their hazelnut, caramel and white chocolate muffins.

"This is amazing," Sarah whispered in awe before taking a sip of her hot chocolate.

Zane smiled proudly at his mom. "My mom has won awards for baking. We used to live in Denver where she had a successful catering business."

Sarah smiled shyly at Gretchen. "I would love to learn how to cook like this."

Gretchen winked at her as she took a sip of her coffee. "Well, I'm looking for afternoon help for the store. If you work for me, I'd be happy to teach you what I know."

Sarah's eyes widened at the possibility. *"Really?* I could work here for you? But what about Zane? Don't you want the job?" she asked, looking back and forth between son and mother.

Gretchen laughed, swinging her long blond hair over her shoulder. "Zane and cooking and cleaning don't go together. Zane's going to be busy doing other things for me," she said looking more serious. "But you're hired if you're interested. I could use you after school from three to six and Saturdays. What do you say?"

Sarah felt a humming start in her toes and work its way to her eyes. She glowed with happiness as she nodded her head. "I would love to. Thanks Gretchen."

"It's settled then. Only one rule to remember. No magic in front of customers."

Sarah's smile faded and she turned to look at Zane accusingly. Zane's mouth was stuffed with muffin, but he shook his head fiercely before reaching for his hot chocolate.

Gretchen reached her hand over the counter and grabbed Sarah's fist. "Honey, Zane didn't have to say one word. The power slap I walked into when I met you told me everything I need to know. Sweetie you gotta learn how to control that energy or you're going to slap everyone silly. People are going to run in the opposite direction if you're not careful."

Sarah groaned and laid her head on her arms. "People do run in the opposite direction of me. I don't know anything about how to control all of this energy I have. And I'm not really comfortable with the term witch. I prefer psychokinesis if you don't mind."

Gretchen stared at Sarah's head in disbelief and then stared at Zane. "Zane, were you power slapped when you two met?"

Zane wiped his mouth with a napkin and grinned at his mother. "No ma'am. For me, it's more like a power magnet than a power slap. I can definitely feel her energy though. I could feel her coming a quarter mile away like she was being pulled to me. She walked into first period and I couldn't believe my eyes. She was lit up brighter than a Christmas tree. But no power slap. It freaks everyone else out though. Everyone except this weird kid named Lash. He

29

seems immune to it for some reason and he's not even a witch," he said not looking happy about it.

Gretchen looked back and forth between Zane and Sarah. "Well, isn't that interesting."

Zane grinned at his mom and reached for a second muffin. "It certainly is. And might I point out she's beautiful."

Gretchen laughed and shook her head at her son. "I've got eyes Zane. You better watch it or you're going to scare her to death."

Sarah raised her head tiredly from her arms. "He did. He does. But I'm slowly getting used to it."

Gretchen laughed and wiped down the counter. "So tell me about yourself Sarah. Who are your people? I grew up here so I should know your parents."

Sarah cleared her throat and looked at Zane nervously. He just looked at her curiously as he munched away.

"Lena Hudson is my aunt. My mom was Rachel Hudson. She died of pancreatic cancer when I was around five and I don't have a father," she said robotically, wincing as she watched Gretchen's face turn solemn.

"Rachel Hudson was your mother?"

Sarah wrapped her cold hands around the warm mug and closed her eyes. "I take it you knew my mom?"

Gretchen frowned and looked down at her feet. "There were a few witch families in the area back then. My family the Adams, the Clearwater family who lived twenty miles out of town and the Ashfords up on the hill. You have to inherit the gene that gives you the gift. I knew your mom and aunt growing up and they aren't witches, which means you had to have inherited your gift through your father's family. The only male witch around back then was Race Livingston. Is Race your dad? He came in the book store just a few hours ago, asking about my

30

mom. We didn't have time to catch up but he looks about the same. He's still very powerful. Just like you," she said, looking at Sarah closely.

Sarah's face went white and she stood up, walking slowly towards the window. "*Race Livingston?* No way," she said, her voice cracking.

Race Livingston was a loner who lived by himself at the edge of town in a large house. Everyone thought he was really weird. Some kids claimed he was a serial killer hiding out and other's thought he had mental problems. *That's who might be her father?*

Zane moved quickly to her side, taking her hand. The warmth Zane gave her, wrapped around her like a cocoon, comforting her and giving her strength at the same time. Gretchen moved out from behind the counter and came to stand on the other side of her.

"You didn't know? You really don't know who your father is?" she said with a perplexed look on her face.

Sarah leaned her face against the window and traced a star pattern. "I've never been told who my real father is. His name isn't even on my birth certificate. All my aunt would ever tell me is that he lives around here, but that for some important reason, I shouldn't know him."

Gretchen and Zane shared surprised looks over her head. "Honey, come sit down. Let's figure this out," she said and turned the sign to CLOSED before motioning Zane and Sarah to a couch by the fireplace.

"Tell me everything," Gretchen commanded and pointed to the couch as Sarah looked nervously at her.

Sarah sighed tiredly and wasn't surprised when Zane sat right next to her, his hand firmly holding hers.

"There's not much to tell. I grew up just like any other normal kid until I was about thirteen. That's when I knew I was different and that I could do things that other people couldn't. It was at that point that I started giving off this weird protective barrier. I noticed

31

people would wince when they got too close. By the time I was fifteen I no longer had any friends. Some days it's stronger. And I've noticed that some people are more affected by it than others. When I turned seventeen last year, my aunt told me that she and I were witches and that I would need to accept my destiny and all this mumbo jumbo crap."

Gretchen snorted. "Lena was always an idiot. Sorry, keep going," she said, wincing at Zane's frown.

Sarah picked a piece of lint off her jeans, ignoring Gretchen's comment. "She's been getting really pushy about being a witch lately. She has these meetings once a week where three other ladies and this super icky guy come over and when they leave, the house feels dark and heavy and horrible. I can't stand to even be in the house sometimes. On some nights, it's so bad I sleep out in the woods behind my house in an old abandoned tree house. I don't feel very safe in my house anymore. I feel like I'm being watched even though no one's there. I feel like something is waiting for me. Something dark and bad," she said, shivering and feeling sick to her stomach as she finally voiced how she felt.

Gretchen pursed her lips and pulled her feet up under her long cotton skirt while Zane put his arm around Sarah's shoulder, making her feel safe and warm.

"Has your aunt ever brought up Race's name?" Gretchen asked curiously not commenting on her aunt's activities.

Sarah shook her head. "No, never. When I was fourteen we had a huge fight about it. I insisted on knowing who he was. I mean, all I knew was that it was a man who lived here in town. I wanted to know so badly because, I mean, if I started to like a boy, I didn't want it to be my brother or cousin or something gross like that."

Gretchen smiled and nodded her head. "I see your point. But she wouldn't tell you, huh?"

Sarah shook her head and played with Zane's ring on his right hand. It felt soothing for some reason.

"The harder I pushed the more determined she was to hold his name back from me. All she would say was that it was for my own good."

Gretchen nodded her head and took a sip out of her cup as she thought about everything she had just heard. "Well, I'd say you have a right to know who your father is and that your father has a right to know his daughter. But that's not really my business. What seems strange to me is that your aunt would tell you that she's a witch. People don't just become witches out of the blue. You're born with it or you're not. And she was not."

Sarah shook her head in confusion. "But I didn't even know I was different until I was a teenager."

Gretchen shook her head. "Every witch comes into their power when they're teenagers. Rarely you'll see someone exhibit power before the age of ten. But even babies have a power stamp. A little hum they emit. Sarah, close your eyes and concentrate. Reach out with your mind and try to sense me and Zane. What do you feel?"

Sarah did what she was told and closed her eyes. She let go of Zane's hand so she could concentrate and moved her energy out of herself and towards Gretchen. She reached her with her mind and felt a warm haze of sunshine. She did the same to Zane and felt something hotter and brighter. She opened her eyes and smiled.

"I could feel you. But I can sense other people too and they're not witches. This boy at school, Lash, I always seem to know exactly where he is."

Gretchen rubbed her forehead with her hand. "Okay, first of all, you weren't sensing me; you just reached out with your energy and *connected* to me. That's very different and that's very rare Sarah. Not many witches can do that. Most witches can sense, but they can't connect. Zane is the only other witch I know who can. I've never been able to."

Sarah turned and stared at Zane. "So when you wrap around me the way you do, that's rare? Is that what I just did to you?"

Zane swallowed and looked at her intently, his eyes bright and gleaming. "Yes, the same way you did this morning when you pushed back at me through your foot. That's why I was so excited about getting to know you."

Sarah tore her eyes away from Zane and took a breath. She decided to think about that later and looked back at Gretchen. "So I can connect but I can't sense? What's wrong with me?"

Gretchen sighed and looked up at the ceiling. "Maybe we're making this too complicated. Think hard Sarah. When you're with your Aunt, what do you feel or sense in comparison to what you feel or sense with me?"

Sarah closed her eyes and leaned her head back against the couch. "When I'm with my aunt, I just feel cornered and poked. Not physically, but like she's pushing on me or pulling on me. But I don't feel a light. I just feel, kind of nothing. With you, I feel like you warm the air around you."

Gretchen smiled and nodded. "That's a good description. Witches let off a power around them that does just that. Warm the air around them. Only another witch can sense that warmth."

Sarah smiled and opened her eyes. "Okay, I can do this." And then she frowned. "Those people my mom invites over to the house, they're not witches either then. Why would they call themselves witches if they're not? And they're always wanting me to join them for their meetings. It's like they're waiting for me to do something, or like they want something from me."

Gretchen frowned worriedly. "Sarah, I don't want to freak you out, but I've known of regular people trying to harness a witch's power. It usually destroys the witch or breaks her into darkness. And the people who are willing to sacrifice a witch's soul just for power? They're predators."

Sarah looked away from Gretchen's compassion and worry and stared up at the picture of the ocean above the fireplace instead. Lena, *a predator*? Would her aunt use her like that? She closed her eyes and felt lonely and cold. She wouldn't put it past her.

Chapter 4 - Shadows

Sarah had Zane drop her off a block away from her house. He was visibly irritated by her insistence, but she held firm. She didn't want to answer questions about him just yet. Her aunt wouldn't like it that's for sure. She hated Sarah being connected to anyone but her.

She walked up to the older red brick rambler with black shutters and opened the door. The blast of darkness that hit her as soon as she stepped over the threshold had her putting her arms across her stomach protectively. She swallowed nervously as Gretchen's words ran through her mind for the hundredth time. Her aunt's friends were here to use her and change her. And she didn't want anything to do with it.

She heard low murmurs coming from the kitchen as she walked softly down the hallway towards her room. She shut the door quickly and grabbed a book, her favorite blanket and some clean jeans and a sweater. She shoved it all in her back pack and slowly opened her door. She saw movement down the hallway and held her breath.

"I think I heard the front door Lena. I hope Sarah's ready tonight because I don't want to wait any longer," a man's voice said, carrying down the hallway on a stream of excitement.

Sarah eased away from the door and turned her bedroom light off. She quickly moved to her window and slid it open. She jumped the three feet to the flower bed below and turned to stare up at the window. She closed her eyes, concentrating on the feel of metal in her mind and heard the window shut itself. She smiled in satisfaction. Her smile turned into a grimace of annoyance though as someone turned the light on in her room. She sprinted quickly away and into the shadows.

She had been brutally honest with her aunt about not being a part of her group of friends or joining in any of their activities. Before when Lena demanded to know where she went at night, Sarah had told her she went to Jill Cavanaugh's to do homework. On nights she stayed out all night, she told her she was sleeping over. But really, she escaped to the woods. Most kids her age wouldn't understand wanting to be in a dark and spooky forest rather than in a nice home. But most kids didn't understand what evil really felt like. She did. She knew and she hated it.

She jogged lightly down the street and towards the woods. She felt a soft buzzing in her ears and glanced around slowing to a walk. The buzzing turned into a light flutter that settled in her chest. All of her senses went on high alert and she could feel the adrenaline being released into her blood stream. Her breath started coming fast as she walked towards the last home on the street. She blended into the shadows and calmed her breathing as she scanned the street over and over wondering what had tripped her senses. She eased back even further and hunched down over her feet and waited.

A shadow pulled away from a house halfway down the street. She watched it curiously as it moved slowly down the sidewalk. It paused looking down the road and towards the woods but then changed course and moved quickly in the opposite direction towards town. She closed her eyes and sent her energy out towards this entity. Her energy reached the shadow and she felt a deep, dark blackness. Her energy scattered instinctively so she brought it back. She watched until she couldn't see the shadow move at all. When her heart rate slowed and her energy was calm she pulled away from the house and ran for the trees. She would be safe now.

Chapter 5 - Just Friends

Sarah walked into first period just as the tardy bell sounded. She smiled at Zane who was already sitting down and collapsed in her chair as she tried to hide her yawn.

"Late night huh?" Zane said softly as Mr. Terrence started handing out papers.

Sarah winced and nodded. "You could say that."

Zane frowned worriedly but let it go as Mr. Terrence handed them both the course syllabus.

Mr. Terrence spent the rest of the class right in front of her and Zane lecturing so there was no chance for conversation. But as soon as class was over, Zane grabbed her hand and pulled her outside the school to sit on the front steps.

"I'm going to be late to Calculus," she protested.

Zane rolled his eyes. "So get a tardy. Now tell me what happened after I dropped you off. I knew I should have gone into the house with you. I need to know what you're dealing with Sarah. Did they do anything last night? Did that guy you were telling us about pressure you into doing something?" he asked tightly, looking more and more upset.

Sarah shook her head quickly and reached out to touch his arm, sending a comforting wave through Zane automatically. Zane relaxed and clasped her hand in his.

"No, it was nothing like that. I snuck in and they were all in the kitchen. But it felt horrible. *Dark*. It's never felt that bad before. It was like this overwhelming bleakness mixed in with evil. So I grabbed some stuff out of my room and jumped out the window. I spent the night in the woods," she said with a frown as she heard the bell for the next class.

Zane pulled her up and they walked back into the school together. "That's not exactly safe either Sarah. Come to the bookstore. We have an extra room you can sleep in."

Sarah smiled gratefully up at Zane as the hallway began to thin out. "That's sweet Zane, but I don't know if I'm ready to move in with you just yet."

Zane grinned and slung an arm around her shoulder. "Give me one more week and you'll be more than ready."

"*Sarah.*"

Sarah turned around, causing Zane's arm to fall away. Lash was standing in the shadow between the lockers and the custodian's closet. He stared at her intently as he walked towards her ignoring Zane.

"Hi Lash," she said, blushing as he looked her up and down in a blatantly admiring way. She did some looking herself and noticed he looked even better than he had yesterday. He was wearing dark jeans and a form fitting gray v neck t-shirt that accentuated his new physique. He moved in close to her and grabbed her hand blocking out Zane.

"I was wondering if you had plans this Friday. We could catch a movie and then go back to my house."

Sarah felt her heart warm as Lash tried his best to dazzle her. He had come a long way. She found herself honestly tempted to say yes, but something held her back. He looked amazing, almost like he could be a member of a boy band with his dark, carefree hair and bright blue eyes. Her smile dimmed as he confidently waited for her answer. There was something dark in his eyes behind his new charisma. Something that shouldn't be there.

"Lash, as much fun as that sounds, I'm going to have to say no. Jill was my science partner and I consider her a friend. You guys looked pretty close yesterday and I don't want to cause any problems."

Zane sighed loudly and walked a few steps away to lean against a locker. He took out his phone and scanned through his texts but at the same time she felt a strong warm breeze wrapped around her torso and move up the back of her neck. She tried to ignore it and looked back in time to see Lash's smile turn into a disappointed frown.

"Sarah, Jill is just a friend. You and I have had a connection ever since I moved here. I do . . . *need* to be with Jill sometimes, but every time I'm with her, it just makes me want to be with you even more. I told you yesterday I would give you some time to think about the two of us, but the more I think about it, the more I like the idea. I don't really want to wait anymore. I think we should start going out."

Sarah's eyebrows went up an inch in surprise and her mouth opened. "Uhhh . . ."

Zane moved away from the locker and came to stand next to her sliding his phone into his back pocket. "Hi, I'm Zane," he said, extending his hand towards Lash.

Lash tore his eyes away from Sarah and turned impatiently towards Zane. "Yeah, I'm aware," he said staring at Zane's hand for an awkward moment before taking it. He looked almost angrily at Zane and then instead of letting go, stepped closer, squeezing tighter and tighter. Zane raised an eyebrow derisively but then shrugged and squeezed back.

"Look, I know you just moved here Zane, but me and Sarah have a history that you couldn't understand. We've cared about each other too long to have some surfer show up and ruin everything."

Zane's face turned from friendly to hard as the muscles in his arms bunched. Sarah switched her gaze to Lash's face and noticed that not only were the muscles bunched in his arm too, but he was gritting his teeth and looking like he wanted to kill Zane.

Zane shook his head, still trying to squeeze the life out of Lash. "There's caring and then there's caring. I'm sure the way Sarah feels about you is *very* different than how she feels about me. Don't take it too hard Lash. And just for the record, I don't surf."

Lash bared his teeth at Zane as his other hand turned into a fist.

"That's enough guys. I insist you stop right now," she said putting her hand over theirs and feeling the brutal effort they were both putting into crushing each other's bones.

Zane's eyes turned silver and she felt a burst of energy shoot through him and into Lash causing him to gasp in pain and immediately let go of Zane's hand.

"Whatever you say Sarah," Zane said, putting his arm back around her shoulders.

She stared at Zane reproachfully but wasn't sure she disagreed with the way he handled Lash. Lash seemed determined to be aggressive.

"But to answer your question Lash, Sarah already has plans Friday night. She's working at the book store and then having dinner with me and my mom. Sorry buddy," he said, not unkindly

Lash flexed his hand and looked at Sarah as if he was hurt. "Seriously Sarah? *This* guy? You've never let a guy get close to you before," he said, sounding confused.

Sarah tried to push Zane's arm off, but gave up and reached out for Lash's hand. She concentrated her energy on the pain she could feel coursing through his nerve endings and pulled it out of his skin and into the air. Lash's face relaxed as the pain disappeared and he looked pleadingly at her.

"Lash, Zane and I are friends. *Just* friends, right now. I think you're sweet to want to go out with me, but like I said, this situation is too messy for me. Something is different about you now. I'm worried about you Lash. Something's not right. Please tell me what's going on."

Lash looked surprised and massaged his hand, ignoring Zane again. "You wouldn't understand Sarah. I'm doing this for the both of us. You know I would never hurt you, right?"

Sarah blinked in surprise. "Of course you wouldn't. Why would you say that?"

Lash shook his head, looking sad for a moment. "I just mean that out of everyone in this world, I would never want to hurt you. You mean more to me than anyone."

Sarah's eyes softened and she stepped forward and gave Lash a hug, putting her arms around him and squeezing warmly. It was the first hug she'd ever given him. Lash's arms immediately wrapped around her, holding her more tightly than she expected. She could feel raw emotion pouring out of Lash and stepped back in surprise. Lash refused to let go at first, but then slowly released his arms.

"*Lash,*" Sarah said, shaking her head as he leaned his head against her shoulder for a moment before pulling away.

Lash stared for a moment at Zane and then turned and walked quickly down the hallway, leaving Sarah and Zane completely alone.

Sarah let her breath out slowly and rubbed the goose bumps off her arms. "Oh my heck. What just happened?"

Zane stood silently staring after Lash, not saying anything. Sarah bumped her hip into his and grabbed his arm. "Come on Zane. We're both going to get a tardy now. Let's go."

Zane shook his head with a frown and then put his hand on the small of her back. "Okay, but before I wash this little scene from my mind with bleach, you have to admit that was a little bit much, don't you think?"

Sarah frowned and looked away as they walked quickly towards the other end of the school. "It was so sweet and sad at the same time. I guess I kind of understand why he would feel that way about me. I've been the only one in almost ten years to be nice to him. But he seemed kind of desperate. I could feel it in his voice. He needs me for something. It almost feels like he needs my help."

Zane snorted rudely and moved his hand up to the back of her neck, sending streams of warmth down her spine soothing her. She smiled up at him gratefully.

"Yesterday was the first time I've seen Lash and every time he's around you, he looks at you like you're a Thanksgiving meal and he hasn't had anything to eat in a week. That crap about not wanting to hurt you? It sounds like he's trying to convince himself. That guy is dangerous Sarah. I don't want you going out with him," he said in a deadly serious voice.

Sarah stopped in her tracks and turned to stare up at Zane's cold metallic eyes. "Did you just say what I think you said? No, of course you wouldn't be telling me who to date. That'd be kind of strange coming from a guy *I just met yesterday*."

Zane's eyes turned angry and he stepped away from her for the first time since they'd met. "I'm just a guy you happened to meet yesterday? Fine Sarah. Have it your way."

Sarah felt ill as she watched Zane turn and walk away from her, taking all the warmth with him. She was left with the remainder of her goose bumps and an empty lonely feeling.

"*Great*," she grumbled and walked into calculus. She zoned out what her teacher said and didn't even flinch when she was sent to the office for being tardy.

Three hours later, as she took her lunch tray and scanned the cafeteria for an empty table she felt a strong warmth wrap around her middle and actually pull her to her right. She gasped and stumbled as she felt jerked towards the farthest table. She frowned in consternation as Zane's strong back and his wavy dark blond hair came into view.

She shook her head but moved of her own free will to sit down next to him. Zane ignored her and smiled up at Charity Klein, the daughter of the Mayor.

"I'd love to Charity, but Sarah has plans for me Friday. She wouldn't tell me what we're doing, but I'm kind of excited to go out on our first date."

Charity blinked in surprise and turned to stare at Sarah in displeasure. "You're dating *her*? Please tell me you're kidding," she said looking sincerely confused.

Zane shrugged and turned away from Charity to face Sarah. "I know, I was surprised too. The most beautiful girl in school, practically throwing herself at me. What can I say, I'm a lucky guy."

Sarah raised an eyebrow as Charity walked away in a huff. "I *threw* myself at you?" Zane sat back in his chair, crossing his arms over his chest and stared at her coolly. "Am I really just some guy you met yesterday, Sarah?"

Sarah dropped her eyes to the Hawaiian Haystack on her plate and pushed the rice and pineapple around and around with her fork. "Well, yes and no. Yes, you are a guy I met yesterday. But then you're also the guy who knows me better after one day than anyone else has after a lifetime. Look, I'm sorry I hurt your feelings this morning, but I care about Lash. That doesn't mean I want to date him, at least I don't think so. But he might need me and you don't have the right to tell me who I can and can't spend time with," she said quietly, but firmly, still not looking at him.

Zane took her fork out of her hands and took a bite of her lunch. "This is disgusting. Eat this instead," he said, pushing one of his mom's muffins across the table.

Sarah glanced up cautiously and took the muffin, peeling back the foil slowly. The smell of nutmeg, cinnamon and apples flooded her senses and she smiled.

"Thank you," she said, taking a decadent bite of the glazed muffin.

Zane watched her as she closed her eyes in pleasure and gave her a half smile. "So let's settle this then. You and I have a connection. Because we're both witches, or because I'm attracted to you, or because it's a combination of both, who knows and I don't care. It doesn't matter because the bottom line is, *we're connected*. I can understand that you're also connected to Lash. From what I gather, it's a protective bond that's been created over time. But he wants to change that connection to a romantic one and you're too smart not to realize that. But here's the problem. Because I'm already connected to you, I don't want Lash connected to you at all. Mostly because I can see something in him that tells me he's a danger to you. I care about you Sarah. I already care about you, enough to know that I don't want you hurt," he said in a deep, serious voice that she'd never heard him use before.

Sarah swallowed her bite of muffin and pushed the rest away as she took in what Zane was telling her. She licked her lips and took a sip of her chocolate milk.

44

"I agree with most of what you said and I understand it. But I can't just ignore this bond I have with Lash because you're not comfortable with it. I know Lash wants a more romantic relationship with me, but that's not going to happen. *Unless I want it to,*" she added softly.

Zane sat up straighter and narrowed his eyes at her. "Pity is not a good basis for a relationship you know. Mutual strength and compatibility win every time. You don't really want some strange, sick co-dependent relationship do you?"

Sarah shook her head in frustration. "Stop psycho-analyzing this Zane. The point is, I don't know what's going to happen. I like you. I like Lash. I like you both for different reasons, true, but it's still there."

Zane frowned and tore off a chunk of her muffin. "You really want a guy who just got back from doing who knows what to Jill Cavanaugh? She's been dating him, what? For a week? And she already looks used up and half dead. That's the guy you're considering going out with instead of me?"

Sarah turned her head to see what Zane was looking at and saw Lash and Jill come through the side doors. Zane was right. Jill didn't look good. The smile on her face looked strange and faded and she looked pale. Her usually glossy brown hair looked dull and mousy and her bright, brown eyes were almost colorless. Lash had a possessive arm around her shoulders and a content look on his face. She knew in her gut what they'd been doing. Lash paused for a second and scanned the room, stopping when he found her face. Sarah looked back, curious as to why just that morning he'd ask her out when something physical was going on between him and Jill.

Lash tilted his head, ignoring Jill pulling on his arm and smiled warmly and almost sweetly back at her. He raised a hand in a half wave and then gave in to Jill's pulling and followed her to the lunch line.

Zane's hand on her chin pulled her face back to him. "You don't want to be a part of that Sarah. I don't want to see that happen to you. If you dated him, it would."

45

Sarah looked back into Zane's clear gray eyes and realized he had moved his chair closer to hers. They were hip to hip now and his hand on her chin was sending a wave of warmth down her body. She didn't try to move away when he moved in closer.

"I don't know . . .," she managed to say before Zane moved his face a few inches closer and kissed her.

Sarah's mind went blank as Zane moved in, kissing her in a frank, possessive way that had the sounds of the lunchroom immediately fading. It was her first kiss and she didn't want to miss a second of it. Almost against her will, her energy swelled up out of her and surrounded Zane as her arms reached up around his neck, pulling him closer. She leaned in, letting her energy envelope them in a protective field. A moment later, she was disappointed when Zane broke the kiss.

Sarah opened her eyes, to see Zane staring down at her, dazed. She stared back up at him noticing that his gray eyes were bright silver again and that she could almost see a golden haze shimmering around him. They stared at each other silently for a moment before she pulled her arms from around his neck. The golden haze around Zane slowly faded until the air was normal and she could hear the chatter and noise of the people surrounding them again.

Zane reached up and touched her lower lip with his finger. "You can't deny our connection."

Sarah swallowed and realized that her energy was still surrounding Zane. She pulled it back almost by force. He looked disappointed she had. "Why would I want to?"

Zane smiled and leaned in again but was stopped by the sound of Lash and Rod screaming at each other. Sarah stood up at the same time Zane did just in time to see Lash go flying over a chair to land in a heap. Before she could even move, Lash was up and diving for Rod. The fist fight was short lived but brutal. Rod outweighed Lash by a good thirty pounds, but Lash's relentless fists had Rod on the ground almost immediately. Three male teachers surrounded the fight and it took all three teachers to restrain Lash. Two of them cornered Lash until he calmed down while the other teacher helped Rod to his feet. Rod limped through the doors with the help of Mr. Terrence while Lash sauntered by Sarah and Zane, escorted by Mr. Jones, the Vice principle and Mr. McAllister the football coach. As he passed them, he stared at Sarah closely and then turned to glare at Zane, pointing his finger like a gun at him.

Zane and Sarah sat back down when the doors swung closed and looked at each other. "Okay," she said, not knowing what else to say.

Zane shrugged and grinned a little. "You do look like you've just been kissed."

Sarah blushed and rubbed her hand over her lips. "*Really*?"

Zane nodded with a smile. "Don't worry. I'm a lot harder to take down than Rod."

Sarah groaned and grabbed her tray, standing up. "Zane, please don't fight with Lash. I don't understand what's going on with him so instead of fighting, let's figure out how we can help him."

Zane took the tray from her and put his arm around her shoulders. "I would never throw the first punch. I'm not that stupid."

Sarah looked up at him suspiciously. "You look like you'd throw the second, third and fourth though."

Zane dumped their garbage and then opened the door for her. "You are very perceptive Sarah. I like that about you."

Chapter 6 - Binding

Sarah accepted a ride home from Zane since she had to be at work by three. She waved goodbye to him and ignored his request for a good bye kiss with a laugh. She felt him leave and walked slowly up the pathway to her front door. She paused before opening the door with the bright cheery sign on the front that said, *Welcome*. She felt a wave of darkness hit her, but it wasn't half as strong as it had been the other night. She stepped cautiously through the door and came face to face with her aunt.

"I've been waiting for you Sarah," Lena said, looking sternly at her, her hair looking spiky as if she had run her hands through it, over and over again.

Sarah slipped her back pack off her shoulder and sat down on the couch. "Okay, what's up?" she asked in a polite, calm way.

Lena's eyes narrowed at her as she sat in the chair opposite her niece. "I expected you at the meeting last night. We all did. We waited for you until after one o'clock in the morning. You let me down and I won't have it Sarah. You're my niece and you'll do what I say."

Sarah took in a deep breath and looked down at her plain finger nails. "I was very clear with you that I want nothing to do with your meetings. I'll never go to your meetings Lena. So let it go."

Lena's cheeks turned bright red and her foot started tapping. "You don't know what you're missing Sarah. You have to give it at least one chance before you turn me down. How can you say no when you don't know anything about what we do? You need to learn how to be a witch Sarah. How else will you learn unless I teach you?" she asked sounding rational.

Sarah felt the strain of the atmosphere wrap around her head, pushing in like a nail. "How can someone who isn't a witch, teach me?" she asked quietly, knowing suddenly it was true.

Lena gasped and stared at her in shock. "Who have you been talking to? Why would you say that to me? Of course I'm a witch. It runs in families."

Sarah massaged her forehead before answering. "Gretchen Miner. She says she knew you when you were both growing up and she says no way you're a witch. So what exactly are you playing at with these people every week? What are you doing that makes the house feel so dark? And who is my father? If he's a witch, I have a few questions for him," she said, watching curiously as Lena's face turned paler and paler and her foot tapped faster and faster.

"Gretchen Miner doesn't know one thing about me," Lena hissed, looking furious.

"Lena, it doesn't really matter if I'm a witch or I have a whole bunch of psychokinesis. It all comes down to the same thing. I can do some things other people can't and I can sense things about people. I was around Gretchen and now I know what another witch feels like. I can sense that. Lena, you're *not* a witch. So why are you doing this?" she asked sadly.

Lena stood up and grabbed a small emerald green vase off the coffee table and threw it as hard as she could at the wall. Sarah held her arms out and sent her energy out instinctively to protect herself from the shards of glass flying everywhere.

Lena stood with her head down and her hands on her waist, breathing heavily. Sarah had never seen her lose control like this before. "Is Race Livingston my father?" she asked standing up and inching towards the door in case her aunt felt like throwing anything else.

Lena raised her head slowly and speared Sarah with her pale eyes. "I won't talk about your father. Not now, not ever. I don't care what Gretchen has been telling you, she doesn't know as much as she thinks she does. Power is power and if you'll just come to my meeting, Drake can explain it to you. It's called a binding. You bind yourself to us and then we can guide you. You'll be even more powerful than you are now and I'll be able to share it with you. Drake knows exactly what to do. He's done it before and he says you're perfect for this. He says I'll finally have the life I've always deserved," Lena said, in a pleading voice.

Sarah's face contorted in pain. Gretchen had been right. Her aunt had gotten sucked in to a group that was determined to use her and break her.

"My answer would have to be no then. And if you want me to keep living here, you'll stop inviting your friends over. Now I just got a part time job at the book store, so I've gotta run. I don't know when I'll be home so lock up and I'll use the key," she said, standing up and walking towards the door.

Lena darted forward and grabbed her arm, pulling her to a standstill. "I've done everything for you Sarah. I've sacrificed so much of my life for you. And you won't do this one thing for me? I've never asked you for anything Sarah. This is very important to me. If you love me you'll do this," she asked in a wheedling voice.

Sarah felt a mass of darkness from the corner of the room glide over and float next to her aunt. She couldn't see a form, but she could feel the energy outline. She felt the dark energy start to flow around her, like it was trying to meld with her. She closed her eyes for a second and concentrated on her ever present energy barrier. The darkness couldn't break through. She wouldn't let it.

She pulled her arm out of her aunt's grasp and opened the front door. "I love you enough to tell you that if you don't stop this, you're going to end up a lonely shell. I shouldn't have to live my life in darkness because of your choices."

Lena glared at her niece as she walked out the door. She shut the door slowly and leaned her head against the cool metal as the dark energy folded itself around her.

Chapter 7 - Power Slap

Sarah ran down the street as fast as she could. The faster she ran the cooler and cleaner the air felt. Two blocks later she could breathe easier and she slowed down. She moved her energy over her body and around in a fast circular motion almost as if she were trying the scrub herself clean. Being touched by that evil made her want to puke. She shivered and ran her hands through her long red hair. *What was happening to her aunt?* She barely recognized the woman who had just thrown the vase at the wall because she wasn't getting her way.

Sarah glanced at her watch and saw that she had ten minutes before she needed to be at the book store. She slowed to a walk and shoved her hands in her pockets, breathing deeply and praying for calm. But it was no use. Her energy was in turmoil because of the evil that had tried to touch her. Her hair was starting to go from wavy to curly and she knew if she looked in a mirror her eyes would be too bright and her energy would be too hot for anyone to get close to her. This had happened only a few times before since she'd turned thirteen and all three times had been when she'd felt she was in danger.

Sarah wrapped her arms around her torso and walked over to a shop window. She leaned against the window for a moment, pretending she was looking at all of the baby clothes and toys. Instead, she closed her eyes and tried to push some of her energy out into the air. If she could get rid of some of it, she might not have to scare all of the customers away. She didn't want to get fired on her first day of work. Gretchen had been very clear. No magic around customers. Or in her case, enough energy to power the city for a week.

She wasn't sure if she could control herself. A year ago, after an especially vicious fight over her power, she had burst every light bulb in the house. The microwave stopped working and they'd had to buy a new computer.

Sarah breathed in and out and tried to gather her energy again, but it was too volatile. She couldn't control it when her emotions were overloaded. If she could just go for a five mile run or a swim she'd be able to contain it a little. She could feel her power spiraling inside of her, getting further and further out of control like a tornado.

"Hey Sarah!"

Sarah groaned and opened her eyes, fisting her hands and turning to see who was calling, hoping they wouldn't notice her burning eyes. She shaded her eyes and saw a man getting out of a parked car about five feet away.

She watched cautiously as the man walked up to her, stopping a foot away. He was tall with short brownish hair and a large beer belly. He had colorless eyes and a big smile. He wore the basic adult male uniform of her town, polo shirt, tan pants and tennis shoes. He held a hand out to shake.

"I've wanted to meet you forever Sarah. Your aunt has told me so much about you," he said still holding his hand out to her.

She knew if she shook his hand, he'd get hurt. She was surprised that he wasn't bouncing off her energy barrier as it was. She stepped back from him and shook her head warningly. He lowered his hand and frowned at her.

"My name is Drake Conway. I'm a close friend of Lena's. I'd like to be a good friend to you too," he said trying to come closer. Sarah frowned and stepped back again.

"I was just talking to my aunt about that. I don't want to be friends with you and I don't want you coming over to my house ever again. Stay away from us," she said, her voice breaking when a spike of energy ripped through her.

Sarah heard a strange cracking noise and glanced at the window she had been pretending to look through just a moment before. A long jagged scar was forming in the glass. If she didn't move away quickly, the window was going to shatter.

She moved around Drake and started walking away. He fell in step with her and she immediately felt a wave of darkness try to attach itself to her and she shivered.

"There's no reason to act like this Sarah. I'm sure once you get to know me and hear me out, you'll agree that you and I and your Aunt are going to have a very long and productive relationship."

Sarah looked at Drake, aghast that he'd even think such a thing. His eyes were bright and he looked excited. She realized that he had her between himself and his car and felt a moment's panic. Her senses were so fried she'd barely noticed the adrenaline rushing through her system. He reached out to grab her arm and she went on instinct. Her energy converged and tightened around her and when Drake's hand touched her, it shattered around his hand, making him scream in pain.

She reared back from him and almost fell into his car, since the passenger door had been left open. Drake fell onto the sidewalk staring at his hand in horror and still screeching. She shuddered as she eased around him and turned to walk backwards. He tried to roll to his side, but cried out in agony. He turned to stare at her, getting up on his knees, holding up his hand to her. She gasped as she could see it had turned bright red and purple.

"Sarah!" he screamed after her.

She turned and ran into what felt like a brick wall. She almost fell down but was grasped by two warm hands that immediately pulled her in close to a hard chest. She sighed in relief. *Zane.*

"What's going on Sarah?" Zane demanded tightly, staring at the man still holding his hand and moaning loudly.

Sarah glanced back at Drake and shuddered. "That's the man who's been coming to my aunt's house. He just tried to talk to me and then he grabbed my arm. I think I fried him," she said, turning back into his chest, searching for some warmth.

Zane made a low sound in the back of his throat and set her back from him. Sarah felt cold as she watched him advance towards Drake. Zane pulled Drake up to his knees and threw him against his car. He got close to his face and talked in a low voice she couldn't hear. Drake swallowed and shook his head back and forth. Zane grabbed Drake's injured hand making the man squeal loudly. Zane said something else and then stepped away. He turned and walked back to her without looking back.

Zane took her by the shoulders and looked closely into her face. "I could feel you three blocks away Sarah. You've got so much energy pulsing around you, you're about to start flying."

Sarah groaned and felt her hands begin to shake. "I know, when I get like this, I can't control it. I just keep spiraling up and up until I find a release for all of this energy. I don't know what to do Zane. I'm supposed to be at work right now."

Zane nodded and took out his phone. He called his mom and put an arm around her shoulders sending his warm breeze around her body trying to calm her down. Instead it just made her hair crackle and kink and her body shake even more.

"My mom says to take an hour and then come in. Let's go. Where do you feel safest?"

"My tree house."

"Let's go there," he said. "Can I take my jeep there or should we walk?"

Sarah shuddered and glanced back at Drake who was now sitting in his car, staring at her and muttering to himself.

"Both. Drive down Bracken Street and you can park it at the end by the last house. No one lives there anymore so it's okay. We can run the rest of the way."

Zane helped her into the car and joined her a moment later. Sarah closed her eyes and concentrated on her breathing. She tried reciting the alphabet over and over but even that did nothing.

Zane stopped the car a few minutes later and she opened her eyes. "Let's run," she said and jumped out of the jeep. She felt the energy she had been trying as hard as she could to hold back whip through her body and scream out her fingers. She flew down the road and into the trees, feeling the energy crest in her shoulders and pour down her back. She leaped over a log and ducked under a branch before she headed down the path that was so familiar to her.

She looked to her left and felt her heart ease when she saw Zane running right with her. He glanced over at her, looking worried. She put on more speed hoping that would help and reached the tree house much too quickly.

She came to a stop by the large maple tree still shaking from the power. She leaned against the tree as Zane came to a stop in front of her. She stared back at him, as their breath slowed down. His eyes were silver again and he stepped closer. "I can take a little energy off your hands. Give what you can to me," he said and leaned in, settling his mouth against hers.

The same thing that happened at lunch happened again. Her power whipped through her body and out, surrounding him. He seemed impervious to the energy, as if he soaked it in. As he kissed her, her arms snaked around his back, holding him tight. His hands came up to her face to hold her head gently. She felt her body sigh and relax. She pulled back, staring up into his eyes and then kissed him gently one more time.

"Thank you," she said quietly, leaning her head against his chest.

He wrapped his arms around her protectively, rubbing circles on her back. "Kissing you is not a chore. But you're welcome." He tilted her chin up, looking over her face carefully. "Now tell me what set you off."

Sarah smoothed her hair back and sighed, letting the last of the excess energy seep out into the wind. "Come on," she said and turned towards the tree. She rubbed her hands on her pants and then jumped up to grab the lowest hanging branch. She flipped her body up and over and then hitched her leg over. She pulled herself up and then grabbed the next branch. Four more branches later, she crawled into a small tree house someone had built many years ago and then abandoned. It had a roof and a floor and that was about it. Her sleeping bag and pillow were covered with leaves and twigs. She sat down and waited for Zane to join her.

He landed beside her and showed her a cut on his hand. "Your tree attacked me," he said with a shake of his head.

Sarah took his palm in her hand and rubbed her thumb over the blood and closed her eyes. She sent a pulse of energy through her hand to his and rubbed his palm again, back and forth. She opened her eyes and looked down. The blood was still there, but the cut had closed.

Zane studied his hand, touching it was his finger. "Cool. It felt hot where you touched me, but the pain left. Thanks. I guess we know what your special talent is. That and running."

Sarah grinned and leaned her head on his shoulder. "Sometimes it works, sometimes it doesn't. Sometimes I can't control it at all and sometimes it works without me wanting it too. That part scares me."

Zane nodded in understanding and put his arm around her shoulders. "Tell me what happened."

Sarah went over her confrontation with her aunt and what Drake had said to her. Zane didn't say a word until she was done.

"Well, I don't think you're safe at home. But Sarah, its September now. It's going to get cold fast. You won't be able to hide out in the woods much longer. And you shouldn't have to. What if Drake found you out here by yourself sleeping? I don't like it. Do you have any other relatives that live in town?" he asked, leaning down and kissing the top of her head absently.

Sarah shook her head and played with his ring on his finger, feeling peaceful and safe. "My mother died when I was five, around the same time as my grandmother. My aunt mentioned a long time ago that I have cousins in Minneapolis, but I've never met them. Next year I'll go away to college, but for now I think I'm stuck."

Zane shook his head. "No, we'll figure it out. When do you turn eighteen?"

Sarah looked up and shrugged. "I'm already eighteen. My Aunt started me in school late. She held me back a year. I'm legally an adult."

Zane grinned. "I don't turn eighteen until December. I'm holding an older woman in my arms. This day just keeps getting better and better. But the best thing is, you can legally move out any time you want. This is perfect."

Sarah groaned. "Yeah, my life is so perfect."

Zane stood up, crouching down so he didn't hit his head on the little roof. "Come on, we gotta get you to work before your boss fires you."

She followed him down the tree, and floated down from the last branch. She loved the feel of the air pushing her from below. She landed next to Zane as he stared at her with a grin. "Now that's gotta come in handy," he said as wrapped his arms around her. "Maybe I should kiss you one more time, just to make sure you're okay?"

Sarah laughed and felt normal again. "If this is how you act on Tuesday what are you going to be like on Friday?"

Zane swooped in and kissed her quickly. "Well, I'm pretty sure you're taking me out on a date."

Sarah grinned and shook her head. "That's right, I threw myself at you. I'd forgotten about that. Come on, let's run back," she said and took off leaving Zane by her tree.

Zane caught up with her halfway to the car and passed her up. Sarah focused all her energy into her legs and caught up with him quickly. They reached the car at the same time, panting and grinning. Zane opened the door for her and shook his head. "No one's been able to catch me in years. You're incredibly fast. You could get a scholarship to run track, easy."

Sarah shrugged and grabbed her seat belt. "I guess I better start thinking about that. Maybe you're right. It's time to think about my future and life after high school."

They drove quickly through town and arrived at the book store minutes later. Gretchen opened the door to them, looking worried. Sarah glanced around the book store and noticed only two elderly men in the back of the store reading guidebooks.

"Come sit down and drink some hot chocolate. You both look drained."

Zane raised his eyebrow at her behind his mom's back, making her blush. Sarah ignored Zane and took the mug of steaming chocolate Gretchen pushed into her hands, sitting down tiredly. She had just told Zane everything and didn't think she could do it again. She looked at Zane pleadingly and he nodded his head in understanding. He told his mom word for word everything she had told him. But when he got to the part where he grabbed Drake's hand, she perked up.

"What *did* you say to him Zane?" Sarah asked, leaning her head on her hand.

Zane shrugged and looked uncomfortable. "I might have mentioned to him that he was weak and pathetic and that if he came near you again he'd be walking with a limp the rest of his life."

Sarah remembered the horrified look she'd seen on Drake's face as Zane had threatened him.

Gretchen pursed her lips and began to say something but then changed her mind as her two customers walked up to the register. She walked off quickly, leaving Zane and Sarah alone.

"Thanks for coming to my rescue Zane. I might not have had the chance to mention it to you, but your moving here has been about the best thing that's happened in a very long time," she said, not looking at him.

Zane pushed her hot chocolate away and scooted closer to her, bringing her in for a hug. "We're even then. Your walking into English class yesterday is still burned into my mind as one of the best moments of my life. And rescuing you is just a perk. It gives me something to look forward to every day."

Sarah laughed softly and reached up to play with the hair over his ear and then yanked on it playfully. "You know, I'm not exactly a damsel in distress. I had the situation completely under control before you showed up. But it's still nice to know you're looking out for me. I've never had that before. I have to admit, you're growing on me."

Zane's eyes turned soft and he leaned in to kiss her softly on her cheek. "Good, you're falling right into my trap then."

The door rattled and the bell rang as the men walked out with their purchases. Zane looked around curiously as a different man walked in. Zane stiffened and pulled away from her, turning his body to block her from view. Sarah peeked around his arm and noticed the man was tall, with black hair that swept his collar. He was dressed in a business suit and looked wealthy and strangely familiar. His handsome face was smooth and he could have been anywhere from thirty to fifty. He had an older feel to him that contrasted with his young face though.

"Would you happen to have any books on ancient rituals?" he asked Gretchen.

Gretchen shook her head firmly. "Sorry, we're more into the basics. Fiction and guide books and cook books with the occasional book on bird watching and dinosaurs. You might want to try Jasper's in the city. I know the owner and he carries a diverse selection. I can give you his name if you have a moment," she said sounding helpful, but looking grim.

The man shook his head. "No need. I know just the man you're talking about. Thanks for the information. Good day to you," he said and walked out the door.

Gretchen rubbed her arms quickly and then moved to re-join them at the counter.

"Mom, who was that? His aura was slimier than that guy Drake's this afternoon. He was practically shouting death," Zane said sounding sincerely worried.

Gretchen nodded her head in agreement. "I don't think I've ever felt anything so dark before. I hope he doesn't come back."

Sarah looked back and forth between the mother and son. "I don't get this whole aura thing. Why can you see auras and I can't? I just saw a rich guy who needed a haircut."

Gretchen looked at her curiously. "Well, it is strange. You might not have a feel for auras but you do have a highly developed sense of danger. If someone means you harm, your senses are already five steps ahead of you. And I have a feeling that that power slap you give everybody is just you subconsciously protecting yourself. I still don't know why it doesn't work on Zane, but I'll figure it out. In the meantime, I don't think I'd worry about it. We've got more pressing matters to deal with right now. Like your living situation. I don't feel good sending you back home. But I can't invite you to move in with us either, much as Zane would love it," she said shaking her head at her son reprovingly.

Zane blushed and got busy drinking his hot chocolate. "The greater good mom. Let's keep that in mind."

Sarah held up her hand. "It's okay. I'm not here to dump my problems on you. I've been living with my aunt since I was five. I can handle it and when I can't, then I go to the woods. I have some time before it gets too cold. I'll be okay. I'm here because you hired me to do a job not beg for a place to live."

Gretchen smiled at her and put her hands on her hips. "Well, too bad because I know the perfect situation. There's a small apartment above the store. Zane and I live with my mom so we can keep an eye on her at night. Her daytime nurse leaves at 6:30, so we need to be there in case she wanders off. But I'd be happy to let you live in the little room upstairs. It's got a small kitchenette and a tiny bathroom. It has hot water and it's safe. What do you say?"

Sarah's face lit up and she smiled at Gretchen. "I'd have to say thank you. From the bottom of my heart, thank you. This could make my last year of school bearable."

Gretchen reached over the counter and patted her hand. "My pleasure. I'm going to keep my eye on you. You're something special Sarah and I think one of the reasons Zane and I were meant to move here was because of you."

Zane nodded his head in agreement. "Remember your dream mom? The one about the lost girl? It has to be Sarah."

Gretchen paused and stared at Zane for a moment caught in her thoughts and then turned and studied Sarah closely. She reached out and touched the back of Sarah's hand lightly, closing her eyes for a moment. She opened them slowly looking pensive and serious. "I don't know Zane. It's not clear yet."

Sarah was curious about the dream but didn't know if she was ready for any more problems. If Gretchen was having dreams about her, it couldn't be anything good.

Gretchen patted her hand comfortingly. "Let's not worry about that just yet. Right now let's teach you how to stock shelves if you're up to it."

Sarah nodded her head, eager to earn her keep and spent the rest of the afternoon stocking the new children's section.

That night after locking up the store and saying good night to Zane and Gretchen she made a quick phone call to her aunt. She told her that she had decided to move out and that she would come home later in the week to collect her things. She hung up the phone sadly as her aunt started screeching at her hysterically.

She turned the power off on her cell phone and walked into the small bedroom. She glanced over the window seat and the cheerful quilt Gretchen had just barely laid on the bed and sighed all the way from the bottom of her feet to her heart. She closed her eyes and sent her energy out of herself bringing it slowly back a moment later. The room was clean just like the bookstore. No evil lurked here, waiting to stare at her from the corners of the room. She was safe. She smiled as she felt hints of Agnes Adams. Agnes had always had such a comforting, peaceful feel to her and she could still sense that in the room.

After washing her face and brushing her teeth with the toothbrush Gretchen had given her, she turned off the light and got into bed. She usually stayed awake as long as possible to keep the dark things back, but she knew this night there was no need.

Chapter 8 - Talents

Sarah woke up the next day feeling more refreshed and peaceful than she had in years. She stood up and walked to the window, raising the blinds and staring out at the cool September morning. For the first time in a long time she realized how beautiful her town was and that she was grateful to be there.

She took a quick shower but then had no choice but to wear the same jeans she had worn yesterday. She slipped the t-shirt Gretchen had given to her last night over her head and grinned, enjoying the picture of the wizard on the front and the words, *Release the Wizard Within*. It was obviously a well-beloved t-shirt left over from The Lord of the Rings craze.

She glanced at her face critically, wishing for some cover up and lip gloss but knew there was nothing she could do about it. She ran down the staircase and opened the door to the bookstore. She walked into the well lit room and over to the front counter where Gretchen was already hard at work going over the receipts.

"Hey there. Wow, a good night's rest has done wonders for you. And wait just a second," she said, walking around the counter and coming within two feet of her. She held a cautious hand out, reaching very slowly out to touch her arm. "It's softer," she said wonderingly.

Sarah looked at her curiously. "What?"

Gretchen smiled and tapped her chin. "Your power slap. I've been thinking about your energy field a lot. I have a theory about it and this might prove me right. You didn't have to sleep in a house filled with evil last night. Hence, you're energy isn't concentrated on the outside, busy protecting you. The evil was ever present so your field was too. But now? Now you're approachable. Of course I'd hate to see what happens when someone really tried to harm you. Zane's description of what happened to that man's hand was fascinating. But I wonder what would happen if someone tried something worse. You're the most interesting witch I've ever met Sarah," Gretchen said in wonderment.

Sarah blushed and shoved her hands in her jean pockets. "I've done a lot of research on the internet. If it weren't for Google and all the research done on paranormal abilities I'd be a basket case. I don't think of myself as a witch. I really prefer to call it psychokinesis. There's a wide spectrum of power. In the past, people were labeled as witches for having psychokinesis. They didn't understand it and thought it was some evil power. Most people just use ten to fifteen percent of their brain. I just happen to use more of it. Just like you and Zane."

Gretchen grinned at her and turned to go back behind the counter. "Zane's right. You're darling. Okay, we'll just say you have psychokinesis for now. But I will agree with you about the past. Anything people didn't understand or felt threatened by was immediately called evil. When in reality the majority of witches were very good people who helped and looked out for others and were protectors and healers. But there is evil in the world and evil loves power. That's why witches, or in your case, *people who have psychokinesis*, have to be always on guard to protect themselves from those who would use them and eventually destroy them."

Sarah nodded her head readily. "I think you're right Gretchen. I've always looked out for the kids at school who are bullied. It's like I can't help myself. I have to step in and protect them."

Gretchen nodded her head in understanding. "I can feel that about you. You're a healer and protector. Zane's more the warrior, which is actually centered in protecting others as well. I'm glad to know that you two will have each other's backs."

Sarah blushed and looked away. It was weird discussing Zane with his mom. Her feelings for him were turning into something she wasn't even sure how to describe yet.

"Sarah, do you mind if I ask you what powers you do have? I'm very curious."

Sarah straightened the gum and the candy bars as she thought about it. "Well, sometimes I can read minds. Not exactly word for word or anything like that, but I can tell what people are thinking and feeling. Usually when it's directed at me, or at someone trying to hurt someone I want to protect. I can't really go up to any random person and tell what they're thinking. I have to be connected somehow."

Gretchen looked intrigued, but motioned for her to go on. Sarah squinched up her nose and thought about everything she could do. "You know about my energy field. You said Zane has it too. He uses his differently though. He can reach out so easily. Yesterday, he was half way across the cafeteria and he physically pulled me towards him. I even stumbled a little it was so powerful. But people are drawn to him. He described it as being a porch light and normal people are moths. I'm not a porch light though. I'm more of a human taser."

Gretchen laughed. "Zane, Zane," she muttered trying to sound reproving, but sounding amused instead. "Well, you have to understand that he grew up with me for a mom. I knew he was a witch just a few months after getting pregnant with him. I was about six months pregnant when I first felt him wrap his energy around me. Most witches, like I told you the other day, don't show their power until their teen years. Zane has had bursts of power throughout his entire life. He's one of the most powerful witches I know. But he's also one of the best. His heart is so strong and good. He's going to do amazing things in his life. I can feel it. But yes, he knows how to use his energy and he enjoys doing it. But don't discount yourself Sarah. You've been using your energy by instinct or subconsciously. There's power in that too. We'll take some time this weekend to help you learn how to fully pull in the energy so there's no power slap. But there are times, when you're going to want to slap someone. We'll teach you that too. What else you got?"

Sarah felt strange actually talking about her powers with someone as if it were normal. But it felt amazing too. "I can heal people. I can draw pain out of their bodies and I can close wounds. At least that's all I've tried to do. I don't know if I can do more than that. I think it takes necessity for my power to work."

Gretchen nodded. "Of course. What else?"

64

Sarah looked away, almost nervous about what she was going to say. "Sometimes when I'm running, I almost float. And when I was hiding out from my aunt in the garage one time, I felt she was coming so I snuck out the window. The drop off under that window is at least 7 feet. I knew I'd break my leg or ankle if I jumped, so I floated down. I could feel the wind drive up under my body, slowing me down. I could feel it pushing on me. And when I run, I can feel it lifting me sometimes."

Gretchen looked intrigued. "I've heard of that power before but I never believed it was real. That's amazing Sarah. Honestly amazing. And what about yesterday? Zane mentioned that your energy was getting out of control. So much happened yesterday that I didn't get the chance to talk to you about it, but describe what happened."

Sarah bit her lip feeling insecure. "When I get really upset, like yesterday, my power spirals out of control until I can find an outlet for it. It was kind of scary to be honest. Usually I can go for a run and that helps. But yesterday was different. It was too much for me to control. I cracked the glass in a store window and even frying Drake's hand didn't help. Zane and I ran through the forest and then he . . .," Sarah stopped and looked away in embarrassment.

Gretchen frowned and motioned with her hand. "Go on, what did Zane do that helped?"

Sarah blushed a bright red and looked down at her feet, wishing the subject had never come up. "He kissed me. When he kissed me, all my energy, kind of zoomed up and out of me and surrounded Zane and he kind of just absorbed it. He took what I couldn't handle and it didn't even hurt him. He didn't seem to have a bad reaction to it."

Gretchen's eyes widened and her eyebrows raised half way up her forehead. "*Oookaaay . . .*"

Sarah held up her hand. "I know, this is weird and I feel very uncomfortable telling you about that kiss. I'm sorry."

Gretchen shook her head and laughed. "Hey, I used to be a teenager a long time ago. I'm not judging you. But the fact that he was able to absorb that much of your energy without any harm or side effects is not only strange, it's miraculous. I have no way to explain it."

Sarah sighed and held up her hands. "Please don't try. Let's just pretend that we never discussed it."

Gretchen laughed in real amusement and shook her head. "That's a deal. But just know that you can talk to me about anything. Anything to do with your powers. Anything to do with anything. You haven't had the most normal life so far. I want to help you Sarah. Like you, I'm a protector and I feel like I'm here to guide you. I have a good feeling about you."

Sarah smiled and felt excited for the first time about her powers. No longer was it something to feel strange and different about. She wasn't alone anymore. She was going to learn how to control what she'd been given. Maybe now she'd have a chance at a normal life.

"Listen, you better run or you're going to be late for school. Look, there's Zane now," she said pointing out the window.

Sarah glanced over her shoulder at Zane's silver jeep and felt warmth pour down her spine and wrap around her. She sighed happily and grabbed her backpack.

"Thanks Gretchen. I'll see you after school."

Gretchen held up a hand. "Don't forget breakfast," she said and handed her a bagel filled with eggs and cheese.

Sarah smiled delightedly. "Zane is so lucky," she said and ran out the door.

Gretchen looked after her with a sad smile and went to turn the sign to OPEN.

Chapter 9 - Blood Lust

Zane leaned over and kissed her cheek when she hopped into the jeep. *"Wow.* You look so beautiful today," he said sounding in awe.

Sarah blushed and lowered the mirror to look at herself. All she saw was her same face, make up free. *"Riiiight,"* she said doubtfully.

Zane grinned and drove away from the curb. "Trust me on this."

Sarah relaxed and watched the town go by and found herself smiling. She felt so alive today almost carefree. She honestly couldn't remember the last time she'd felt so good. It was almost as if she'd come out of a dark scary cave and out into the sunlight. It felt amazing.

"Listen Sarah, I'm going to drop you off and then head over to your house to get your things. Mom and I talked about it last night and we both think it'd be safer if I went by myself while you're aunt is at work. No drama and it can be done and you won't have to worry about it."

Sarah frowned and grabbed Zane's hand. "I don't think that's a good idea Zane. I'm coming with you. What if my aunt catches you? What if Drakes there? I don't want you to get hurt," she said worriedly.

Zane looked at her in surprise and laughed. He reached over and touched her cheek, sending a warm pulse through her skin and down to her heart. "You are absolutely lovely. You're worried about me? Sweetheart, it's them you should be worried about. Trust me."

Sarah studied his confident smiling face and relaxed a little. "Sorry, I forgot for a moment who I was talking to," she said bowing her head to him sarcastically.

Zane laughed again and pulled up in front of the school. "I'll see you at lunch," he promised and leaned over for a kiss.

She looked around at all the kids milling around the parking lot and looked back at him, still patiently waiting for her. "This doesn't mean we're together or anything you know," she said hesitantly.

Zane lifted an eyebrow and Sarah felt his energy wrap around her body. She leaned over and quickly kissed him, but not fast enough to avoid the energy that seeped into her almost immediately.

"You and I will have to agree to disagree for a while on that," Zane said narrowing his eyes at her.

Sarah smiled and opened the door. "I can still get that restraining order you know," she teased.

Zane laughed and pulled the door shut with his energy, leaving her at the curb grinning her head off.

She walked into the school and realized that she already wished it was lunch time. Time went by slowly and when fourth period finally came around, she gave serious thought to skipping. She felt antsy and worried about Zane. She wouldn't be able to relax until she knew he was okay.

Fourth period was her World Civilization's class. The teacher didn't have an assigned seating chart so everyone sat wherever they wanted to. She headed for the back of the class as usual, but changed course when she saw an empty seat behind Jill Cavanaugh. Jill had her head down as if she was studying her textbook, but to Sarah, she looked like she was just too weak to lift her head. Sarah frowned and glanced around the classroom to see if anyone else had noticed the change in Jill. All the other kids were too busy talking, flirting, complaining and doing the usual.

She sat down and leaned forward to tap Jill on the shoulder and stopped with her hand in the air. She slowly lowered her hand as she saw a small drip of blood slowly make its way down the back of Jill's neck. No one would have noticed, but Jill's hair had drifted to the side. Sarah stared at the red liquid, mesmerized and horrified at the same time. She got her book out and set it on the desk opening it, without even caring about what page she was on. She leaned over her book, very similar to the way Jill was, and closed her eyes. She sent her energy out of herself and towards Jill. She wrapped around Jill and concentrated on her neck. She could feel the seeping blood pulsing around a deep laceration. She could feel the dull pain and the weariness in Jill. She probed deeper and felt something even stranger, longing and a complete lack of care for herself. She could tell that Jill didn't even care that she was hurt or that her body was so weakened. She felt in Jill a desire to give up everything she was for what, she didn't know. *But she could guess.* For the first time in her life, she felt anger towards Lash.

She concentrated her energy on the laceration on Jill's neck. She'd only been able to heal in the past by physically touching the wound, but she knew she wouldn't be able to do that this time. Jill would never allow her to. She blocked everything out and felt Jill's blood and her skin. She used all her energy to bring the skin together. She faintly heard the teacher come in, but she knew she needed a few more minutes. The cut was deep and was nothing like the scratch she had taken just moments to heal yesterday on Zane.

"Miss Hudson? Is something wrong?" Mrs. Jensen asked.

Sarah heard her speaking to her through a thick haze and looked up while trying to heal at the same time. It was exhausting and the strain on her face must have shown because Mrs. Jensen looked worried.

"I think you should go see the nurse Sarah," she said walking to her desk to write a note.

Sarah lowered her head again without saying anything in reply and sent out a burst of energy in the hopes of closing the skin on Jill's neck.

Jill slowly turned around to stare at Sarah. She reached back as if to touch her neck but then lowered her hand. *"Sarah?* Are you okay?"

Sarah raised her head and sighed, knowing that even though the skin was closed, it was a very fragile bond. Anything could break it open again. "I'm okay Jill. What about you? You don't look like you're feeling very well either."

Jill shrugged and tried to smile. "Just a bug going around."

Sarah frowned. "Sure."

"Here Sarah. Head to the Nurse's office. You look like you're going to pass out."

Sarah shrugged but took the note and stood up. "I'm okay Mrs. Jensen."

Mrs. Jensen shook her head and motioned to the door with her head. Sarah walked out of the room and shoved the note in her pocket. She and Lash needed to have a little conversation. She closed her eyes and felt for him. She'd never really analyzed why she always knew where he was in school. She'd been able to do that since Junior High. She accredited it to the fact that she'd thought so much about protecting him from bullies that it was just ingrained in her now.

She leaned up against a wall for a moment and then just knew absolutely that he was three doors down the hall. She walked towards the door and looked through the window. She stood at an angle so that the teacher wouldn't be able to see her. She looked around the classroom until she found Lash. He was sitting in the back with his head thrown back and his hands cradling his head. He looked cocky and self-assured and there was a girl leaning towards him, trying to get his attention. He had such a self-satisfied look to him that she felt like hitting him. Just then he looked right at her and his grin faded and turned into a real smile. She motioned for him to come to her with her finger. He immediately raised his hand and walked up to talk to the teacher. He opened the door seconds later and pulled her down the hallway towards the back doors.

"Let's go talk out here. I know the perfect place," he said excitedly.

Sarah glared at his back, but let herself be pulled towards the football field and the bleachers. A few moments later they were standing in quiet privacy. She took a moment to look around and get a feel for the place.

"I get a feeling you come here a lot," Sarah said quietly.

Lash shrugged and leaned against a post. He reached out and ran a hand down a lock of her hair, pulling gently through the waves. "I've always loved your hair Sarah."

Sarah looked down at her feet. "I need to talk to you Lash."

Lash grabbed her hand and pulled her closer. "I knew you would. I knew you couldn't be seriously interested in Zane. I'm so glad you came to get me. You have no idea," he said and then before she knew what he was about, he'd pulled her into his arms and began kissing her as if he'd been dying to.

Sarah squawked in protest and tried to pull back but his arms were like a vice around her. Her energy that automatically wrapped itself around Zane, whenever he kissed her, was rearing up to shatter over Lash. She stomped on his foot hard before she seriously hurt him. She tried to pull her energy back, but some of it seeped out onto Lash, giving him a power slap for the first time since she'd known him.

Lash looked shocked and paralyzed for a moment. He shook his head and rubbed his arms, wincing. "What just happened?" he asked, still feeling pain shooting through his nerve endings.

Sarah could have reached out and taken the pain back, but chose not to. "Don't kiss me like that again Lash. You have to ask first. You can't just dive in and take."

Lash swallowed and looked away. "I thought . . . I thought you came to find me because you wanted me as much as I wanted you," he said sounding confused and hurt.

Sarah shook her head and stepped away from Lash. "I told you we need to talk. I didn't say grab me and shove your tongue down my throat."

Lash looked away in embarrassment and then looked back at her angrily. "Then what is this about, if you don't mind my asking?"

Sarah put her hands on her hips and stared at him coldly. "I saw the back of Jill's neck Lash. I could feel you on her, like you left an imprint. What are you doing to her? It feels like you're draining her. Tell me why she's bleeding Lash," she insisted, staring him down.

Lash whipped his head up, looking at her aghast. "*What?* How do you know that?"

Sarah shook her head in confused disgust. "Tell me or I'll do whatever I have to, to stop you. I won't let you hurt her Lash. The last few days she's gone from beautiful, bright and alive, to dull, exhausted and gray. Tell me right now what you're doing to her."

Lash turned away from her, shoving his hands in his pockets and looking miserable. He walked a few steps away and then turned back. "I don't have a choice. So much was taken from me. He's always taken too much. Like he's had a right to me. Like I was just there for him to use any time he wanted. Like I was just a thing and not a person. I've been so weak my whole life because of him. I figured that if he could take from me, then I could take from someone too. And it worked. I couldn't believe how well it worked. And I finally became the person I was always meant to be, you know. Strong, and powerful. People see me differently now. *I am different.* I'm finally me. Sarah, you have no idea what it's like to be used and used and used. Now it's me using. And I get it."

Sarah shook her head in confusion and grabbed Lash's hand. Not just to steady him, and calm him, but to sense what he was trying to tell her behind the words. Her touch immediately brought his agitation down and he looked her straight in the eyes.

"Sarah, do you know what Blutrausch is?"

Sarah shook her head. "No. I've never heard of it. Tell me."

Lash kept hold of her hand but looked away. "It's blood lust."

Sarah's mouth fell open in horror. "What are you telling me Lash? Are you telling me that you're drinking Jill's blood? What is this, some vampire thing?" she asked, feeling squeamish and physically sickened by the thought.

Lash looked at her in pained silence for a moment. "Yeah, that's what I'm trying to tell you. My mom died when I was seven and ever since then, my dad's been taking my blood. That's why I've always been so weak, and small and unhealthy. He practically drained me dry a few times and he had to take me to the hospital for blood transfusions. One time a doctor got suspicious enough to call Family Services. He suspected my father was abusing me, but my dad just paid the social worker off and it was back to life as I knew it. Or hell more like it. The only bright spot in my life has been you Sarah. You'd look at me and you wouldn't see this used up shell, this victim. You saw *me* and you helped me and protected me. I love you for that Sarah and I will love you until I die."

Sarah felt so ill she slid to the ground, still holding Lash's hand in hers. He kneeled down beside her and tilted his neck and lifted his hair. She looked at the back of his neck at the hundreds of scars crisscrossing his neck and felt tears fall down her cheeks. She lifted a hand to touch his neck, wanting so much to heal the skin, to heal the little boy who was so taken advantage of. She could feel the heat and energy leave her hand and press down into Lash's neck, but it bounced back almost immediately. This she couldn't heal.

Lash raised his head and took her other hand in his. His blue eyes were intense and open and vulnerable. "My father took and took and took from me. But I stopped him. I finally turned the tables on him this summer. I realized that if I could take blood like he does, I could get stronger. I could regain what he'd taken from me. And I did. I met some girls online and met up with them at the mall in the city. And I'd . . . well, I did what I had to do to get what I needed. After a few months, I confronted my father when he came for me and I was able to fight him off. He leaves me alone now. I don't know where he's getting his blood from now. But it's not me. *It'll never be me again,*" he swore looking savage and wild.

Sarah groaned and lowered her head to touch Lash's arm. "I'm so sorry Lash. I'm so sorry."

Lash bent his head and leaned it against hers. "I'm okay now. I'm better than okay now Sarah. When I move out this summer, I'll never have to see my father again. Ever. I hope he dies."

Sarah raised her head at the hatred she heard in Lash's voice. She leaned back from him and raised her hand to touch his cheek. "Lash, it breaks my heart what your father did to you. But what you've done to those girls in the city and what you're doing to Jill now is just as bad. Can't you see that you're just repeating the cycle?"

Lash looked taken aback and blinked a few times. "You don't understand Sarah. I *have* to take the blood now. I need to get stronger. The more blood I take, the better I get. At first, I thought it was disgusting. I had to force myself to do it. I'd get the girl I was with drunk and then I'd make a small slit on the back of her neck, where she wouldn't notice and the first time I did it, I threw up. But I forced myself to keep going. The next day I felt almost human for the first time since I was a kid. I knew then I had to keep doing it. I hated it Sarah. I hated it, but now . . . now, it's almost like I have to have it. It's like a drug now. I guess that's why they call it blood lust," he said sounding strange and far away.

Sarah swallowed and leaned forward turning Lash's face towards her. "You have to stop Lash. You're going to end up killing Jill if you don't. She's so weak now she can barely sit up in her chair. I won't let you take any more blood from her."

Lash looked angry at first but then stared into her eyes for a few silent moments. He finally lowered his head and sighed. "I've wanted to stop. I just can't. I say I will. I know what I'm doing to Jill. When I look at her sometimes, I can see myself when I was a kid trying to go to school after what my father did to me and I feel sick to death. I feel like I've tainted myself. Almost like I'm unclean now."

Sarah breathed in deep and let it out slowly. "If you're unclean now, then there's a way to become clean again. I know it. The first step is to stop though. I'll help you. The way you're talking is like an addict. There is a ton of help for addicts these days. In health class last year, I did a paper on the 12 step program for drug and alcohol addicts. It's the one thing that seems to work. It'll work for you too."

Lash smiled for the first time and looked at her with what she couldn't deny was love in his eyes. "You're so good to me. You've always been so good to me. I'll do it Sarah. Whatever you say, I'll do. If it means I can be with you someday and be clean and whole, I'll do twenty-four steps. I don't even care."

Sarah winced. "Lash, you have to do this for yourself and for all the people you don't want to hurt, like your father hurt you and like you've been hurting Jill. Doing this doesn't mean that you and I will be together."

Lash frowned and rubbed his thumb across her hand. "But that's what I want. That's what I've always wanted. On days when I was too weak to even move because of my dad, I would lay in bed and day dream about one day being able to escape. And you were always there with me. The hope of being with you has kept me alive Sarah. I can't do this without you."

Sarah grasped his arm in her hand. "You won't have to do this alone. I promise I'll be your friend. I can't promise you anything else."

Lash swallowed and nodded his head. "I'll win you over. I'm going to be clean again and you'll want to be with me then. I promise."

Sarah looked away, not knowing what to say. "Lash, is there somewhere you can live, where you won't have to be with your dad? I don't think you should have to live with a man who would use his own son. He's abused you Lash. He's evil."

Lash nodded. "I know. That's what's so scary. I can see him when I look in the mirror sometimes. I hate that. But it's okay. Now that he knows I'll fight him if he tries to take my blood now, he's never home. He works in the city, so he's been staying there. I haven't seen him in a couple months now. I have a housekeeper that keeps the house clean and meals in the fridge. I know she sends reports to my dad about what I'm doing but I don't care. As long as he stays out of my way, I'm fine. If he comes back? What can he do? I'm stronger now. I'll kill him if he ever touches me again."

Sarah felt her heart sicken at the thought, but knew Lash was serious. She didn't know if she blamed him either.

"So this whole blood lust thing. Is that where all the stories of vampires come from?"

Lash stood up, and held her hand, pulling her up to stand beside him. He gave her a half smile and nodded. "You should see my dad's library. It's full of old dusty books about the subject. Not vampires, but Blutrausch . It's been around since the beginning of time. Small groups of men and women who prey on others. When you start drinking blood, it's addicting not because of what it tastes like, but because of what it does to your body. You're stronger, you stay young and you're smarter. Everything you are becomes more. It's like the fountain of youth and steroids without the side effects. The whole myth about the undead and living forever? Bull. But it does sustain your life past the normal range. My dad is in his fifties but he could pass for his early thirties."

Sarah shook her head in wonder. "That is so crazy."

Lash held her hand and looked at her sadly. "Sarah, do you think I'm, . . . gross, or evil now?"

Sarah looked away frowning, not wanting to meet his eyes. Within her was the desire to help and heal and she knew Lash needed healing. From his father's abuse and from his new addiction to blood. But she was still disgusted too.

"Lash, you're not gross. What you've done is gross. You're not evil. What you're doing is and what's been done to you is. But if you keep going down the path you're on. You'll be just like your dad. I would hate that. And I know you would too."

Lash nodded his head, looking determined. "I refuse to be like my dad. I won't be. I was freaked out that you found out. But you've given me hope that there's a way out. I didn't know there was one."

Sarah smiled and patted his back. "I'll go to the library during the next period and get you the information on the 12 steps. Will you start today?"

Lash nodded his head and smiled. "I already have."

Sarah smiled and grabbed Lash's arm. "Come on; let's get back to school before someone thinks we're out here making out or something," she said with a laugh.

Lash frowned. "I wouldn't have a problem with that."

"I would," said a low, angry voice.

Sarah and Lash turned around and stared at Zane. Sarah's eyes widened at the expression on his face. He looked seriously ticked. She remembered what Zane had done to Drake yesterday and stood in front of Lash just in case.

"Zane, we were just talking," she said, holding a hand up defensively as his expression darkened and he looked over her shoulder at Lash.

"Well, I did kiss her," Lash said cockily.

Sarah groaned and reached back and elbowed Lash in the stomach. "Shut up you idiot before Zane rips you in half."

Lash snorted. "You're assuming he could. There's no way."

Zane started forward. "Why don't we find out," he said, his voice sounding as violent as his eyes looked.

Sarah threw herself in front of Zane, pushing against him with all her might. "No Zane. You don't understand what just happened. Lash, take off. I'll talk to you later."

Lash looked like he wanted to stay and fight with Zane, but she shook her head at him pleadingly and he nodded. He turned and walked away without saying another word.

She turned and looked up into Zane's wary eyes and felt tired all of a sudden.

"Please don't look at me like that. I don't deserve it."

Zane turned away from her, crossing his arms across his chest. "Did he kiss you?" he demanded, sounding horribly disappointed.

Sarah walked up behind Zane and wrapped her arms around him from behind, sending her energy out and around him. She felt him relax slightly. "He did kiss me, but I hurt him for it. He still doesn't have feeling in three of his toes and the power slap I gave him was strong enough to fry a few brain cells."

Zane's shoulder's relaxed and he turned around, looking down at her. "He sounded way too happy about that kiss. He didn't sound like he was in pain at all."

Sarah groaned and lifted her face to the sky. "That's because he was having too much fun torturing you over it."

Zane rested his hand on his hip and looked down at his feet. "I could feel you across town. Every day, I can feel you more and more. I can feel your emotions. I can feel your energy. You're embedded in me somehow. I could tell you were upset and mad. And I could feel this anguish coming from you. It was tearing my soul out. I grabbed your stuff, threw it in the jeep and rushed back. I thought something horrible was happening to you. But then I felt this pity and compassion. Like you wanted to wrap yourself around something or someone and protect them from harm. It was so sharp it was painful. It hurt me. Like it was stripping me from the inside out. I jumped out of my jeep and just ran. I came right to you and I found you here with Lash. I didn't know what to think. I know I didn't like it."

Sarah walked up to Zane and threw her arms around his neck, burying her face in his neck. The tears she had tried so hard not to show Lash, ran down her cheeks now. She started sobbing and shaking and immediately felt Zane's energy pulse around her, sending warmth through every nerve ending she had.

"It's okay now. It's okay," Zane soothed her. "What happened Sarah? Tell me what's going on."

Sarah sniffed and waited a few moments to get her tears under control. Without letting Zane go, she told him everything that had happened since she entered her last class. When she finished, she stepped back, to look up into his face.

Zane stared down at her shaking his head. "*Poor kid.* No wonder you've been trying to help him. I feel like finding his dad and tearing him apart," he said lethally.

Sarah let out a shaky breath and nodded her head in complete agreement. "I'm with you on that."

Zane pulled her back toward his chest, rubbing circles on her back. "We'll help him together. I promise I'll do what I can for him, but on one condition. No more kissing. *Ever.*"

Sarah looked up at Zane with a soft look in her eyes. "Do you want to know when my first kiss was?"

Zane looked irritated but shrugged. "Sure, when was your first kiss? And who was it?" he asked menacingly

Sarah smiled. "Yesterday. You were my first kiss."

Zane's face lighted up and he ran his hands down her hair. "Now that is just as it should be."

Sarah grinned. "You know how when I kiss you, my power kind of wraps around you and flows into you?"

Zane nodded, still smiling. "*Mmm hmmm,*" he said, leaning down toward her mouth.

She pushed back, shaking her head. "Let me finish please. Well, when Lash kissed me, and trust me, I didn't have any warning, my energy whipped up and would have seriously hurt him, if I hadn't tried as hard as I could to hold it back."

Zane's eyes widened and he looked up, over her head as he pondered what she had said. "So what you're saying is, you're meant to be my girlfriend and anyone else who tries to make a move on you will suffer bodily harm if not certain death."

Sarah laughed and pulled away from him as she heard the bell ring for lunch. "Well, that's one way to put it. Another way to look at it would be that my energy instinctively see's Lash as a threat because it can sense the bad in the things he's been doing. Maybe when Lash is free from his addiction, he'll be able to kiss me."

Zane frowned and slung his arm across her shoulders. "And maybe not. There's no sense in putting him in harm's way just to test out a theory Sarah. That would be inhumane."

Sarah laughed, feeling the warmth from Zane wrap around her. "Something to consider."

Chapter 10 - Shells

Sarah pretended not to notice when Zane held her hand as they walked into the cafeteria, but the heat pulsing through her arm kept her senses popping. She looked up at him and smiled when she saw the cocky grin. She wouldn't be surprised if she saw the same grin on her face.

They got in the pizza line and found a table quickly. Zane moved their chairs so they could sit side by side. They had a perfect view of the whole cafeteria together.

"So have you ever heard of this blood lust thing?" Sarah asked Zane quietly in case anyone passing by overheard.

Zane finished chewing his bite and shook his head. "Nah, never. I can see how the stories of vampires came from it though. It seriously grosses me out, but hearing about Lash's life and seeing what's happened to him, I sort of get it."

Sarah frowned, shivering at the memory of Lash's neck. "Zane, he showed me his neck. He lifted the hair at the back of his neck and there were hundreds and hundreds of scars. I felt like part of me died with that little boy every time he was abused. I would love to find his dad and make him pay," she said quietly.

Zane looked up at her considering. "I wouldn't say no to that. But I don't want you hurt. Lash's dad sounds like a psychopath. Besides, what could we do? Killing him would be the best thing for everybody, but if we did, then we'd be just as dark as he is."

Sarah nodded her head. "You're right. We need to focus on Lash now. I'm going to print off the 12 step program for him today and help him get started. He's an addict. We just have to get him sober."

Zane stared at a girl across the room and frowned. "Yeah, for Jill's sake at the very least."

Sarah turned and saw Jill standing in a corner, looking pale, weak and miserable. "Why would a girl give so much of herself to a boy? Even to the point that she'd give up everything."

Zane looked at Sarah closely and grabbed her hand, sending comforting warmth streaming into her. She scooted toward Zane and leaned in closer to his side.

"Sarah, some girls are like that. All a boy has to do is say they love her and they give him anything he wants. It's usually not blood, but it's the same thing. They give important pieces of themselves to guys who are just using them. Some of the girls back in Denver were just like Jill except they were able to hide it better. But it was sad to walk through the hallways at school and see empty, miserable shells, just wanting someone to fill that emptiness and looking to the people who were using them for warmth and light that was never coming. They just kept getting emptier and emptier until by the end of the year sometimes, there was just nothing left of them."

Sarah sighed sadly, still staring at Jill and felt her heart break for her. "Maybe there's a 12 step program for that too."

Zane leaned over and kissed the top of her head and then straightened up in surprise. "Lash wouldn't break up with a girl during lunch would he? Please tell me he's not that big of an idiot."

Sarah sat up and winced as she saw Lash standing next to Jill at a careful distance. He had his hands in his front pocket and a guilty expression on his face. She couldn't hear anything he was saying, but by Jill's horrified expression, he was definitely breaking up with her. Jill started crying and reached out for Lash, but he stepped back, letting her hand fall on empty air.

Lash shook his head almost angrily at her and started to look agitated. He turned his head and looked around the lunch room for a minute until he found Sarah's face. He stared at her for a moment and looked more resolved as he turned back to Jill. He talked to her for another moment and then turned and walked out of the lunchroom.

Sarah and Zane exchanged pained expressions. "Maybe I should go talk to her," Sarah said, standing up slowly.

Zane held on to her hand. "Too late," he said as they both watched Jill crumple to the floor. A teacher and three students rushed to her side and carried her out of the room quickly and with little drama.

"She'll be okay," Zane reassured her. "They'll call her parents and she'll go home. After a few days of Lash not taking her blood, her strength will return and hopefully her sanity too."

Sarah frowned, doubting it would be that easy, but at the same time hoping it would be. "I hate seeing her like this. She wants Lash so badly, but losing him is the best thing for her. Why do people want what's bad for them?"

Zane rested his hands on her shoulders and leaned down to whisper in her ear. "Sometimes though, people get exactly what they want and it's amazing."

Sarah felt her heart ease and she turned to smile up at Zane. "I hope so."

Zane leaned down and kissed her quickly, sending sparks along her nerve endings. "You better believe it."

Chapter 11 - 12 Steps

After school, Sarah had to run to catch up with Lash as he walked towards the front doors. She grabbed his arm to get his attention and he jumped almost nervously but smiled when he saw it was her.

"I was terrified it was Jill again."

Sarah frowned sadly. "That's not likely. She collapsed after you walked out of the lunch room. I overheard some girls talking and her mom came and picked her up."

Lash looked pained by the news, but didn't say anything. "I'm just doing what I have to do. You understand, right Sarah? If I stayed with her, there's no way I could stay clean. I know I'd use her and use her, just like my dad."

Sarah grimaced but nodded. "I know. You did her a big favor breaking up with her today. By the way, here," she said, handing him a blue folder.

Lash raised his eyebrows and opened the folder. When he saw the title on the front page, he sighed heavily. "Time to get to work, huh? Beating an addiction will be a piece of cake, right? Look, just 12 little steps. It's going to be so easy."

Sarah looked at him doubtfully. "Addiction isn't going to be easy Lash. You might have to fight the urge for blood the rest of your life. But if it means you'll turn out to be a strong amazing man, the total opposite of your dad, then it'll be worth it. Right?"

Lash sighed again and closed his eyes, looking tired. "I'd do anything not to become my father. I'll go home and look it over. Um, could you do me a favor?" he asked, looking uncomfortable.

Sarah blinked in surprised. "Yeah, sure Lash. What?"

Lash slipped his hand into his back pocket and pulled out a small silver pocket knife. He held it out to her, so she took it automatically.

"That's what I use to get the blood. Could you get rid of it for me? I don't even want to know where it is."

Sarah swallowed her distaste and tried to smile as she slipped it into her pocket. "Of course. I'll do whatever I can to help you."

Sarah patted his arm, feeling the turmoil, pain and regret swimming around Lash's system. She wished she could take it all away for him but knew she couldn't.

"I'm proud of you Lash. I think . . .," Sarah paused and bit her lip. "I think you're pretty amazing."

Lash looked up, his eyes wide in surprise and he smiled at her, his eyes softening as he stared at her. "The feeling is mutual. Gotta run. Here comes Thor."

Sarah turned to see who Lash was talking about and saw Zane walking purposefully towards her with two girls in tow. Zane saw her and rolled his eyes and then winked. Charity stared in a sultry way up at Zane and reached out to grasp his arm possessively. They were close enough so she could hear what they were saying now.

"Zane, I would love it if you'd come to my party this Friday. You're new to the school and it's my duty to make sure you feel welcome. My parents will be out until late and it'll give me a chance to introduce you to everyone. We've got a heated pool and hot tub and my dad's liquor cabinet is always stocked. I promise you'll have fun Zane."

Zane paused and turned to look down into Charity's pretty face. "Ah Charity, that sounds amazing. But my girlfriend is the most jealous woman in the world. Just today Sarah caught me talking to Alicia Parker and she threatened to key my jeep. I wish I could, but for your own safety, I better not. Have fun girls," he said regretfully and walked away from them, leaving their mouths hanging open.

Sarah shook her head as Zane laughed gleefully and swung his arm over her shoulders, pulling her through the front doors of the school.

"You get the biggest kick out of giving me a bad reputation, don't you?" she said laughing along with him.

Zane nodded readily. "I absolutely do."

Zane drove straight to the store and waited while Sarah got out. "Wait, aren't you getting out with me?"

Zane shook his head while the jeep idled. "I've got some stuff to do for my mom. I'll be back for dinner though. Bye beautiful," he said and grabbed the door with his energy, shutting it in her face.

She stared after the jeep with a frown wondering what he was doing for his mom, and why he hadn't told her what it was. She turned to walk into the store but stopped when she felt a blanket of darkness start to wrap itself around her. She gasped in surprise and used all her energy to protect herself. She reached again for the front door, but felt like she was moving in slow motion.

"Sarah, I need to talk to you," Lena said, stepping out of the shadows.

Sarah swallowed and closed her eyes, trying hard to strengthen the shield around her. She thought of Zane and imagined his power wrapped around her and felt better immediately. She opened her eyes and looked at her aunt.

"What do you want to talk about Lena?" Sarah asked in a surprisingly conversational tone.

Lena smiled brightly and stepped closer. "I read the note you left for me and I want to talk to you about moving back home. It's not right that you're not living with me. I'm your guardian. It's my job to take care of you. I'm glad you have a job, but there's no way you can afford an apartment on a part-time salary. Come home Sarah. Tell me where your clothes are, and I'll put everything back while you're working. Then we can go out to dinner and talk things out. I love you Sarah."

Sarah looked away and felt another wave of darkness hit her from behind. She didn't turn to look, but could feel Drake's presence across the street, staring at her malevolently. She flexed her fingers and clenched her fists.

"You *were* my guardian. I'm eighteen now and I'm legally an adult. I have a safe place to stay now and I'm never moving back. Now that I'm living in the light, and I know what it feels like, I can't ever go back to that darkness. Lena, I'll always feel grateful for the way you took me in and raised me when my mom died, but if you want a relationship with me, you'll get all of this darkness out of your life. Stop the meetings. Get Drake and those women out of your life. Find another focus besides using me. Because I won't be used. Not by you, not by anyone."

Lena glared at her, her expression changing from sweet and pleading, to angry and offended.

"It's that boy Drake told me about. This is all because of him I know it. How pathetic. You're giving up reaching your full potential because of a stupid crush. Well, I might let you come home when he dumps you for someone less freaky and prettier. Men are always on the lookout for the next pretty face. You'll be back Sarah and I bet it's sooner than you realize. You're just like your mother. Giving up everything for a man," Lena said with such a look of disgust on her face that Sarah's eyes widened in surprise.

She watched silently, not saying anything in reply as Lena walked across the street and away from her. Sarah turned to watch her aunt get into the passenger side of a parked car and drive away. Sarah rubbed her cold arms and turned back to the book store. It would be easy to ignore everything Lena had said except for what she'd said about her mother. Sarah didn't know the first thing about Rachel Hudson, but Lena's anger had become almost uncontrollable when she'd brought it up. What if her mom did give up everything for a man? And if so, who? And Why?

She opened the door and walked into the light and put it aside. Someday she'd figure it out. Right now, she had to figure out how to work a till.

Chapter 12 - Normal

Zane picked her up after work and drove her to the local Mexican restaurant.

"It's about time I took you on a real date, don't you think?" he said, holding the door open for her.

Sarah grinned happily. "Well, this is my first date, so yes. It's definitely about time."

Zane shook his head. "Thank goodness for your power slap. It would have been a pain to fight every guy in town off."

Sarah snorted and picked up the menu, scanning the entrées gleefully. "Zane, even if I didn't have all this energy to deal with, I still wouldn't have half the population panting after me. I'm too different. I'm not like those girls at school. I'm not anything like Charity or Alicia."

Zane grimaced and picked up his menu. "Thank goodness. You're so much more. I could look at your face all day long. You're fascinating. And you'd have to be dense not to notice that every guy's eyes are on you every time you walk through the door. It's actually starting to get on my nerves," he said sounding, truly annoyed.

Sarah lowered her menu and stared at him in disbelief. "You're making that up. I've caught a few guys staring at me, but it's like you said the other day. People are fascinated by the power and they're not even sure why they're staring. Moths and porch lights, right?"

Zane grimaced and took a sip of water. "I can sense thoughts too as it so happens. Turns out guys don't just stare at you because you're a witch."

Sarah's mouth fell open and she looked away in embarrassment. "Oh."

Zane looked at her grimly. "Yeah. *Oh.* The sad truth is, you're stunning. In more ways than one."

Sarah shook her head and giggled while Zane laughed at his own joke. "That was lame Zane."

They ordered from the waiter and munched on chips and salsa while they waited. Sarah relaxed and smiled as she looked around the restaurant at other couples, families and friends sharing a meal together. "I feel so normal. This is great."

Zane reached over and grabbed her hand. "Witches can have very normal, happy lives. Just watch. From here on out, you're going to be amazed at how much you're going to enjoy life."

Sarah couldn't help smiling at the thought. "And I take it you're going to be a big part of my happy life?"

Zane looked up in surprise. "Well of course. No one else could make you as happy as I can."

Sarah was saved from answering as the waiter brought their entrees. As Sarah pulled the napkin over her lap she glanced out the front window just in time to see Lash walk past with his arm around a girl. She gasped and pushed back from the table to run to the window, pushing past a waiter and squeezing past a woman who must have been in her seventies.

"Excuse me, please," she said, plastering her face to the glass. She stared at Lash's back and the girl he was holding close to his side. She could tell immediately it wasn't Jill and felt a part of her relax. But it looked like Lash's sobriety was going to be short lived. She realized a second later that Zane was standing next to her, staring at the couple walking away from them.

"That's Charity," Zane said in resignation.

Sarah looked up at him, feeling sick to her heart. "I gave him the 12 steps just hours ago and he's already found a replacement for Jill. Why can't he stop?" she demanded as Zane pulled her back to their table and their cooling food.

Zane sat down and motioned for her to do the same. "Sarah, you can't beat this addiction for him. It's kind of all on his shoulders. He's gotta find the strength somewhere, somehow to fight it."

Sarah took a sip of water feeling waves of disappointment and anger tingle along her nerve endings. "But what about Charity?"

Zane frowned and looked back at the now empty window. "She reminds me a lot of the girls I knew back in Denver. But to be fair to Lash, maybe he just asked a cute girl out on a date. We shouldn't just assume that he's with her to use her. He's a teenage guy just like me. Maybe this is him being normal?" Zane asked, smiling hopefully at her.

Sarah winced and tried to smile back. "Yeah. You have a point. But I have a feeling Charity is going to look kind of gray and empty tomorrow morning."

Zane picked up his fork and looked pensive. "If that's the case, then we'll just have to have another chat with Lash. This will stop one way or another. I promise you."

Sarah looked into Zane's eyes, filled with goodness and strength and believed him. She nodded her head and reached under the table to touch her foot to his. The power she sent up Zane's leg and that wrapped around his heart had him grinning at her.

"Now let's forget about everything but you and me. Deal?" Zane asked raising his glass to her.

Sarah smiled and lifted her glass in return. "Deal."

Later that night after Zane had said goodnight and she was getting ready to turn in, she stood by the window in her small bedroom and stared at the lights from across town. She could tell by the pattern, colors and brightness they were police lights. She frowned and wondered what new disaster was unfolding. She leaned against the cool glass and wished that life would be safe for everyone for just one day.

Chapter 13 - Jealousy

The next morning as Sarah stood at her locker with Zane, she noticed a morbid feeling of sadness making its way through the halls. She turned her head and saw the typical groups of kids talking before class started but there was a difference. No one was smiling.

"Zane, what's going on?" she asked worriedly.

Zane scanned the hallway and nodded. "Something's up. Stay here."

Sarah slipped her army green fitted jacket off and slid it into her locker as she watched Zane walk up to a group of guys who were baseball players. Zane talked for a minute and then looked at Bryan Danes who started talking quickly. Bryan was a nice guy who studied hard and already had a baseball scholarship. He looked upset. Zane turned his head to look at her and as their eyes connected she felt something she'd never felt before. She felt words in her mind as if Zane was talking to her. She heard the name, *Jill*.

She blinked a few times in shock and then looked away, shaken as she felt Zane walk back to her. Zane shut her locker for her and then leaned in close to her, putting his hands on her arms.

Sarah looked up into Zane's worried face and spoke first. "What happened to Jill?"

Zane nodded and looked surprised. "How did you know?"

Sarah stepped in closer to Zane's chest as he wrapped his arms more closely around her. She lifted her mouth to his ears so no one else could hear. "You told me in my mind just now. I felt you say her name."

Zane's intake of breath told her how surprised he was.

"You're kidding me," he said sounding in awe.

Sarah lifted her head to look into his eyes and shook her head. "What happened to her?"

Zane rubbed her back and looked away for a moment. "The police found her body in the park at around 9:30 last night. It looks right now like someone assaulted her. Bryan told me she had lost a lot of blood."

Sarah felt herself go cold and she shut her eyes, trying to shut out the thought that Lash had killed Jill. "Zane, Lash wouldn't do that to her. He just broke up with her. He felt horrible for what he'd already taken. It wasn't him," she said, starting to feel agitated.

Zane wrapped his energy around her making Sarah immediately feel warmer. "Sweetheart, I don't want to think Lash did it either. But if Charity turned him down and he was craving blood, things might have gotten out of control. We just don't know yet. I'm not making up my mind until we talk to Lash."

Sarah nodded her head and looked up at Zane, grabbing his arm. "Let's go find him Zane. Right now," she said turning to walk down the hallway but was pulled back gently but firmly.

"Sarah, they have Lash down at the police station. He's being questioned right now. Bryan says he's been there since last night."

Sarah's eyes widened and she groaned. "This is horrible. What can we do?"

Zane looked up as the bell rang for class to start. "Nothing right now. Let's get through school and we'll talk to my mom and figure something out. But in the meantime, I'm going to find Charity and have a little chat with her."

Sarah leaned up and kissed Zane on the cheek smiling in relief. "You are the best," she whispered fervently.

Zane grinned and pulled her in for a real kiss, making her head swim and her energy blossom and spread out, wrapping around the both of them like a warm blanket.

I love kissing you.

Zane pulled back in surprise. "Did you just say that?"

Sarah grinned and nodded her head. "I wondered if it went both ways. I think we've discovered a new power."

Zane shook his head in amazement. "That is the coolest thing I've ever felt. *Amazing*," he said as they walked to class together.

They spent all of first period having a silent discussion on everything from Jill, Lash and Charity, to telepathy and the difference between psychokinesis and being a witch. Sarah was sure she had finally won the argument for a more modern interpretation of their power but changed her mind when she could feel Zane laughing in her mind.

After class, Sarah watched Zane walk away from her down the hallway and was surprised to feel a part of herself being pulled down the hallway with him. Her connection to Zane was getting stronger and stronger every day. She frowned as she wondered if that was what her mother had felt for her father. Would she give up everything for a man?

She felt the words, *Bye beautiful* slip into her mind from Zane as if they had been there all along and she felt a bright warm light spread throughout not just her body, but her soul. She bowed her head for a moment and decided not to answer the question, because she knew she'd never love a man who'd want her to give up everything for him.

After school she waited for Zane by his jeep. She scanned through her messages and saw three new ones from her aunt Lena. She listened to the first one and then deleted all three. Lena was just saying what she had said yesterday over and over in different ways. But it came back every time to the fact that Lena wanted her back and she wanted her to let Drake bind her to them. *Yuck.* Sarah grimaced and scanned the parking lot for Zane for the tenth time. He was taking his sweet time for sure and she wanted to stop by the Police Department to see if they could talk to Lash.

She closed her eyes and sent her energy out of herself, feeling for him and felt a pulse of warmth come from behind her. She turned around and stared at Zane talking to Charity by the Football stadium. She frowned but then watched as he patted Charity on the shoulder and inch back from her. Charity looked up, wiped her eyes and then threw her arms around Zane's neck, sobbing.

Sarah felt jealousy rip through her system. *"That little witch,"* she breathed out softly. She couldn't see Zane's expression, but it better be as horrified as hers was.

Charity didn't look like she was going to let go any time soon and Zane for some reason wasn't ripping her arms off of his neck. Sarah glared at the back of Zane's head and sent a little energy ball out towards him. She closed her eyes for a moment and thought the words into his mind, *'I'm keying your car right this moment'.* She wasn't sure he would be able to hear her thoughts from this range, but it didn't matter, because her power must have reached him quickly. He looked stiff and frozen for a moment and then he stepped quickly away from Charity, rubbing the back of his neck over and over.

Sarah bit her lip and hoped she hadn't hurt him. She watched as Zane talked to Charity for a few more minutes and then turn and walk away from her. As he walked towards the jeep, his eyes were slits of silver and he looked seriously ticked. Sarah swallowed nervously and tried to look innocent. Zane stalked his way through the parking lot and walked slowly around his jeep, his jaw tight and his eyes glittering as he checked the paint job. Sarah wondered if she should slip out of the jeep and make a run for it.

Try it and I'll chase you down, came a voice in her mind.

Sarah winced and crossed her arms over her chest and waited for the ax to fall. She'd had no idea how much power she'd sent out. She'd have to be more careful. If she'd fried him like she had Drake, she'd feel horrible.

Zane got into the jeep and turned to stare at her. "I tell you I'll talk to Charity for you and you zap my neck? *Are you kidding me?* And then, to top it off you threaten my jeep. I don't know if I'm more horrified or surprised," he said quietly.

Sarah couldn't have felt worse. She looked away from Zane and rubbed her arms. "It looked to me like you were enjoying that very long, very intimate hug more than you should. I'm sorry I hurt you. I was mostly teasing. I just wanted you to know I was here. *Seeing the whole thing.*"

Zane sighed and rested his head on the steering wheel. He lifted his hand to massage his neck again and she felt even worse. Sarah reached over and moved his hand out of the way. She rubbed her hand back and forth over Zane's neck and lifted the pain out of his tingling nerve endings. Zane sighed in relief instantly.

"I'm so sorry," she said again, removing her hand from his neck and opened the door to the jeep with the other. She slipped out of the jeep, shutting the door firmly and walked quickly away. She slid between two parked cars and out of view of the jeep. She immediately felt Zane leave the car and start to follow her. She picked up speed and started running for the sidewalk in front of the school as she felt tears start to course down her cheeks. She was so mortified she could die. Zane was shocked and surprised by her inadvertent cruelty. *Just great.* The one person she cared about more than anyone and she'd intentionally hurt him. She shook her head, disgusted with herself and ran faster.

Sarah sensed Zane getting closer so she darted out into the street and crossed. She knew this town better than Zane did. If she could get out of his sight, she'd lose him and get away. Away from him, away from her embarrassment and away from his angry silver eyes.

Zane's thoughts came into her mind softly, *Knock it off Sarah and stop running. Come back so we can talk.* Sarah felt so horrible she pushed her energy outside of herself like a shield and blocked any other communication from Zane. She ran into a small trinket store and walked quickly to the other end and to the side door. There was no way he'd find her now.

She waved at the clerk and then opened the door. She turned and ran right into Zane's chest.

"I told you the very first day that I could feel you walking towards me. I can feel your blood. I know exactly where you are. Stop running from me and don't block me out," he said, pushing her slowly but surely up against the brick wall.

Sarah looked up into Zane's bright silver eyes and looked away, blinking away more tears. "I'm just so sorry," she said, catching a sob that was trying to break loose.

Zane used his body to block her against the wall and leaned down, kissing the tears making their way down her cheeks. He kissed one side of her face and then the other. She stopped crying, but still couldn't look him in the eyes. He leaned down further and kissed her gently. She turned her face away, not understanding how he could go from mad and upset to kissing just moments later.

"Don't be stupid Sarah. Kiss me back," he said quietly.

Sarah shook her head. "I can't. I hurt you."

Zane sighed and tilted her face up to look at him. She was forced to look him in the eyes and saw immediately that all the anger was gone. "It's okay."

Sarah shook her head. "I honestly wasn't trying to hurt you. I was just trying to get your attention."

Zane's mouth quirked up on one side. "But you were mad when you did it, weren't you?"

Sarah wanted to say no, but the truth was, she had been mad that Charity had her arms around Zane. And she was mad at Zane for letting it happen.

"Why did you let her hug you?" she asked quietly, pushing gently on Zane's chest.

He moved back an inch, but didn't budge more than that. "Because the guy she had just been making out with the night before was in jail on suspicion of murder. Wouldn't you be upset?"

Sarah looked away and shrugged. "I guess. I still don't know why out of all the people in the school she chose you to hug."

Zane's eyes twinkled and his mouth turned up as he leaned in again towards her. "You are so jealous."

Sarah turned and glared up at Zane. "You know, I could zap you again don't you?"

Zane grinned down at her and reached up to cup her face in his hands. "You hated hurting me Sarah. I could feel it. I'm sorry I over-reacted. But that hurt like no other. Talk about the shock of a life-time. I don't even want to know how bad you hurt Drake. I almost feel bad for him now."

Sarah sniffed and held her nose up in the air. "Just pray you don't find out then. Look, I've gotta go. I have an after school job I need to be at in fifteen minutes," she said and scooted down the wall and out of his arms.

Zane grabbed her arm and pulled her back into his arms. "Don't run away from me Sarah. *Don't*. Now look at me."

Sarah still felt like crying for some reason, even though he was trying to make things okay. The mortification and the sight of his angry face just wouldn't leave her mind. She looked up into his silver eyes and shook her head. "I can't get over that I hurt you. Not this fast anyways."

Zane kissed her cheek and pushed her hair away from her face. "It's over. It's done. It's forgotten. We've both learned some important lessons. You won't zap me and I won't hug other girls. We're good Sarah. Let it go and be okay now."

Sarah sighed and wanted so much to give in and just hug Zane and accept that warmth he was trying so hard to give her.

Then why don't you? Zane's voice said in her mind.

Sarah looked at him reproachfully but she answered him back. *Because I'm scared now.*

Zane frowned impatiently and gave up waiting for her and kissed her. He pushed her up against the brick wall and let his energy envelop the both of them. The heat and the comfort blasted through all of Sarah's reservations, embarrassment and regret. Her arms went around his neck and she kissed him back with all of the feelings in her heart. Her energy joined his, melding into a power that had Sarah's hair curling tight and Zane's hair changing and becoming blonder.

The door opened beside them and had Zane pulling away. The clerk laughed at their embarrassment as she threw a couple boxes into the recycling bin. "Don't mind me," she said with a grin.

Sarah touched her mouth and stared up at Zane. "Wow."

Zane looked at her intently and grabbed the back of her neck to pull her in for another kiss but Sarah pulled away. "I've really got to get to work," she whispered against his mouth.

Zane nodded and held her hand as they walked out of the side street and back towards the now empty school parking lot.

"We should argue more often I'm thinking," Zane said with a smile.

Sarah shook her head and laughed. "You're insane. I never want to fight with you ever again. I *hate* it," she said passionately as she sidestepped some broken glass.

Zane dropped her hand and put his arm around her shoulders. "All part of a healthy and very normal relationship. It's how we deal with disagreements that make a relationship stronger or weaker. We know we'll disagree and fight. But learning how to deal with it and making things right is the important part. Running away from me is not the answer," Zane said suddenly serious again.

Sarah grimaced, feeling bad again. "I didn't exactly grow up with healthy, normal loving role models to copy. You're going to have to be patient with me Zane."

Zane reached his jeep and opened the door for her. "Patience, I have. What about you?"

Sarah hopped up into the jeep and smiled as Zane leaned in the doorway, his hand on her knee. "I won't run away next time. I promise. So um, what did Charity say about Lash, when she wasn't attacking you?" Sarah asked in a voice that sounded just slightly snotty.

Zane grinned and raised his arms to lean in the through the doorway. "She was with Lash last night. Her parents are out of town on a trip, and she says they made out for a while. She didn't mention he took any blood and I didn't sense any weakness in her. Her arms are actually quite strong believe it or not. She didn't act or look like Jill at all. I don't get the feeling that Lash gave in Sarah. But he did leave around 2 in the morning. So there's no reason for Lash to even be in jail. Charity said she told the police that this morning when they questioned her, but they think she's lying to cover for him. If they have a good forensic team, Lash should be out by this afternoon. He's got an alibi so they can't go forward without evidence or a confession."

Sarah breathed a sigh of relief and relaxed against the seat, letting her head fall back. "Thank Goodness for Charity and Lash's hormones," she said with feeling.

Zane leaned further into the jeep and kissed Sarah's exposed neck. "Speaking of hormones . . .," he murmured softly.

Sarah pushed him away gently. "Do you really want to show up to school with white hair tomorrow?" she asked with an arched brow.

Zane moved back slightly and leaned down and looked in the jeep mirror. He blinked a few times and then grinned delightedly. "I've been wanting to change my look. But why is it your hair is already relaxing but it didn't change color? Why would mine change and not yours?

101

Sarah smirked and pushed him out the door. "Maybe I'm just too much for you to handle?"

Zane laughed and shut the door. He drove her to the book shop but instead of leaving, he walked in with her and talked to his mom in the back room while Sarah helped three customers. After the store emptied, Zane and Gretchen came back out and Gretchen called out for Sarah to join them at the café counter.

"Zane told me a little about Lash last night and he just filled me in. Here, eat this muffin, you look worn out," she said worriedly.

Sarah accepted the chocolate, chocolate chip muffin gratefully and took a bite. Gretchen stared at Zane for a moment and smiled with a shake of her head.

"Wait, did you get highlights? Your hair is three shades lighter today," she said running her hands through her son's hair. She walked around him staring carefully, looking perplexed.

"Please tell me you didn't skip school to get highlights."

Zane's eyes turned silver again as he grinned at Sarah. "I swear on my life I have not been near a beautician or stylist. No chemicals have come anywhere near me. I just happened to get too close to a lot of energy."

Gretchen turned and looked at Sarah with raised eyebrows. "I don't even want to know," she said, holding her hands up defensively.

Sarah cleared her throat in embarrassment and focused on her muffin. "Um, so what should we do about Jill? Charity says no way Lash could have done it. But that means someone else did. A girl I knew and liked was killed last night and her blood was taken. I'm really worried," she said, trying to turn the conversation back to where it should be.

Gretchen sighed unhappily as she wiped down the counter. "I just don't like any of it. I've heard of blood lust before of course, but I've never come across an actual follower, at least not to my knowledge. I heard from just about every customer who came in today all the details of Jill's murder. Something doesn't feel right about this."

Sarah looked up curiously. "You get feelings about things?"

Gretchen shrugged and started pacing back and forth behind the counter. "Oh sure. Most witches do. Dreams and feelings are always right. Sometimes they're hard to understand, but they're always right. And I have a strong feeling right now, that something bigger is going on here. Zane? I think we're going to need to move quicker."

Zane looked concerned but didn't say anything and continued eating. Sarah looked back and forth between mother and son and raised her hand. Gretchen snorted, but paused her pacing.

"What Sarah?"

"What's going on? Zane disappeared yesterday and now you're talking in code. I'm getting the feeling that something is definitely going on, something bigger, right here, with you two," she said looking suspiciously at Zane.

Zane looked back at her and tilted his head to stare. *Really? You're suspicious of me?* he thought into her mind.

Sarah looked back pensively and sent a thought back. *You're hiding something from me. I don't like that.*

Zane looked at his mother who was staring at them in surprise. "Oh my word you were just talking to each other. I could feel the currents but I couldn't hear anything. *Oh my,*" she said and moved around the counter to sit down, shaking her head in surprise.

Sarah looked back at Zane and raised her eyebrows. Zane finished his bite and got up from his seat, walking behind his mother and massaging her shoulders for a minute before walking behind the counter to grab a soft drink. He got Sarah's favorite out without even asking her preference and handed it to her.

"Mom, it turns out that Sarah and I have a connection that allows us to communicate well. Sometimes we talk, sometimes we don't."

Gretchen raised her head and speared her son with a look. "Don't be a smart-aleck Zane. I'm just in shock because none of the witches I know personally are able to do that. I never knew you could Zane. I didn't know you were that strong. I mean I always knew you were strong, but you were never like this before. It's gotta be Sarah. Your connection to her is making you stronger. From what I'm feeling from you, you're at least twice as powerful as you were before we moved here. I wouldn't be surprised if you found out you had even more powers now. This is truly amazing. It's like witch synergy."

Zane looked at Sarah speculatively and smiled slowly at her. "I can't wait to find out what powers pop out next."

Sarah blushed and cleared her throat. "Gretchen, please tell me what you and Zane are up to. I'd like to have all the cards on the table if you don't mind."

Gretchen pursed her lips and looked at Zane intently. Zane nodded his head and his mom sighed. "Zane has certain skills that are very useful. He can manipulate metal and objects like no one I've ever seen which comes in handy when we need to get through locked doors or other types of locks."

Sarah sat up straight and turned to stare at Zane. "Are you guys thieves?" she asked, sounding shocked.

Zane laughed and bowed his head, his shoulders shaking. Gretchen even grinned briefly.

"Um, no. Sorry, I gave you the wrong impression. Zane is doing a little investigating for me. A year before my mom was diagnosed with Alzheimer's, she started having dreams about a dark man who was going to bring pain and havoc to our town. She said the darkness would bring ruin and loss. She tried to find out all she could and I think she got close too. She emailed me a week before she was found lost and wandering in the woods. She said that she had found the source of darkness and that she was going to do everything she could to stop it. And that was the last we heard from her. The next week, I got a phone call from Dennis Green, the Police Chief. He'd picked her up after a passerby saw her walking in a circle by the edge of the forest. She was malnourished, dehydrated and very anemic. But worse than that, she couldn't remember who she was. She didn't know her name or where she lived or anything. I flew out that same day and after reading through all her notes and emails and seeing what had happened to her, I knew it was time Zane and I moved back. I, *we* . . . both think someone harmed my mom because she got too close to the truth. Zane's been going through all the information my mom left to try and find this darkness. He can break in to anything and with his skill with computers, he's the best paranormal investigator I know," she said proudly with a twinkle in her eye.

Sarah took in a deep breath and stared worriedly at Zane. "It just sounds so dangerous Gretchen. What if someone catches Zane? What if he gets hurt like Agnes?"

Zane reached over and grabbed her hand, but didn't say anything. Sarah felt the warmth and comfort but ignored it as she turned to pin Gretchen with her eyes.

Gretchen nodded her head as she looked at her son. "You have a valid point. But there are two things in our favor. This darkness, or whoever is going to cause all of this pain, doesn't know we're on to him or her. Plus, Zane is more than able to handle himself with anyone. I don't worry about Zane. I worry more for anyone who would try to hurt him."

Sarah closed her eyes and groaned. She stood up in agitation and turned away from Gretchen. "But whoever it was hurt Agnes. And I wasn't even trying to hurt Zane and I hurt him quite badly today. He's not invincible."

Gretchen's head came up in surprise and she turned and looked at Zane questioningly. "She was able to hurt you? How?" she demanded.

Zane shrugged and stood up, coming to stand by Sarah's side, pulling her into a hug. "She happened to see a girl wrapped around me and over reacted just a little. She sent out a little ball of energy in my direction. It hit me from behind and almost took me down. She didn't realize how powerful it was, probably because she was angry when she did it. But yeah, if she was seriously trying to do harm, I would have been in the ER for electrocution."

Gretchen walked around the counter to stand in front of Sarah, looking at her curiously. "Just a little ball, huh?"

Sarah felt miserable again, feeling all of the guilt and mortification come crashing back. Zane squeezed her tighter and thought into her mind. *Let it go Sarah. You're still learning and I'm fine. My mom won't hold it against you. She's more impressed than anything.*

Sarah looked up into Zane's face and tried to smile.

"You're doing it again," Gretchen said with a shake of her head and a small smile. "That's going to get irritating. But to ease your mind, there's not anyone like you around that could hurt him. At least not that I know of," she said, sounding unsure all of a sudden.

"Mom, you're not telling her the other part. Tell her about the dream *you* keep having," Zane said, rubbing Sarah's shoulders.

Gretchen sighed and straightened a magazine. "Being a witch means you always have dreams. Some are more important than others, but this one won't leave me alone and I think it has something to do with my mom and this darkness and why we're here. About once a month for the last year, I've dreamed of a lost witch. She's running as fast as she can through a forest and then all of a sudden, she's flying. But a dark man comes out of the trees and grabs her and she starts falling and falling. The night turns as bright as day and then she's lost forever. I can't find her and I can't reach her. And then I wake up."

Sarah's eyes widened as she remembered all the times she had been running through the forest. "Did the girl look like me?" she whispered, clearing her throat when her voice cracked.

Gretchen shook her head. "It doesn't work like that. When I dream, I become the girl. I can't see myself; I can only feel the total terror and feelings of horror. But for some reason I know this witch is lost. She needs to be found and she needs to be protected. Zane is positive it's you. He mentioned running with you through the forest the other day. I'm not sure though. Believe it or not, there are a few other witches in town. They're all in their thirties and forties now, but there are other possibilities."

Zane snorted and shook his head. "You told me you felt young in your dream. You told me that when you ran you could feel your muscles sing and your long red hair whip your face as you turned to see what was chasing you. It has to be Sarah. She's the only witch with red hair in town. I've checked. Why are you fighting the truth?" Zane demanded sounding irritated.

Gretchen threw her arms into the air, looking upset too. "Because I don't want it to be her! I was caught and I fell into darkness. I wasn't helped or saved. I don't want that to be Sarah. What if I can't protect her? What then? What will happen to you now that you're connected? Talk about darkness," she muttered and walked back around the counter and grabbed a Dr. Pepper out of the fridge.

Zane frowned darkly and looked out the window. "I'll protect her mom. No one will hurt her. And no one will hurt me either," he said, feeling Sarah stiffen in his arms.

Sarah pushed out of Zane's arms and walked a few feet away. "So what if I am the lost witch in your dream? What am I lost from? You started having the dreams before you came here. Are they still the same?"

Gretchen looked up at the celling considering. "They have changed a little. Now when I'm the witch, I'm running with someone beside me. But the great light and the falling still happen every time. But to answer your question about being lost from something. That I don't know for certain. But knowing a little of your background, I would have to guess that you're either lost from your heritage or lost from your father."

Sarah put her hands on her waist and looked down at her feet in thought. "All of this has to be tied together somehow. Your mom getting Alzheimer's, her dreams about the darkness, your dreams about me and then Lash and Jill. Maybe this has something to do with Lash's dad?"

Zane sat back down on his chair but turned it to look at Sarah. "Or it has something to do with Drake and your aunt. Maybe they tried to bind my grandma and it destroyed her mind instead of doing what they wanted it to," he said darkly.

Sarah looked up and felt ill at the thought. "I was just assuming they're crazy occultists or something. But to actually harm someone in the hopes of gaining power, that's just sick."

Gretchen held up her hand. "We're just looking at all the possibilities right now Sarah. That's why Zane is busy after school looking into all the leads we've come up with. But there is one lead we haven't mentioned."

Zane looked up at his mom warningly. "Mom, *don't*."

Gretchen narrowed her eyes at her son and pushed the hair out of her eyes. "You don't think she should know? I disagree, Zane. She needs to be fully protected. Because if she's not, then that leaves you open. Sarah, your father, Race Livingston, still lives in town. There's a possibility that he might have gone dark."

Sarah walked over to her chair and quickly sat down. "You don't know he's my father Gretchen," she whispered looking at her hands.

Gretchen walked over and patted her on the back. "Zane found out yesterday that he is. It's confirmed. He went through Race's house and found the original birth certificate. His name is on it Sarah. The copy Zane found in your aunt's files has been tampered with. Race is your father. And when Zane was in his house, he found a whole room covered with pictures of you. Some as recent as last week."

Sarah winced and looked at Zane, reaching out for his hand. "That scares me."

Zane nodded his head. "Then you're smart. We don't know for sure about your father, but until we do, you keep close to me and my mom and the store. No more running through the forest alone or sleeping in the tree house, okay?"

Sarah nodded her head emphatically and looked over her shoulder as a group of senior citizens came through the door.

Gretchen smiled and patted Sarah on the shoulder. "Time to work. But don't worry about it all too much Sarah. We're stronger now, all of us. We'll figure it all out in time."

Sarah sighed and stood up. Zane pulled her in for a strong, warm hug and then leaned down and kissed her, ignoring the clucks of the older women milling around the store. When he pulled away, he held her face and looked down into her eyes. "We've got each other's backs now Sarah. There's nothing they can do. I want you to have dinner with us tonight. I want you to talk to my grandma. She might have a reaction to seeing you."

Sarah nodded and leaned her head against his chest for a moment before pulling away. "Okay, but please be careful. Promise?"

Zane grinned and pulled on a lock of her red hair before stepping back. "I've got you to think of now. Of course I'll be careful."

Sarah watched Zane walk out of the store and felt sick to her stomach. He hadn't even told her where he was going.

"Miss? Where are the books on romance?"

Sarah smiled and walked over to show the lady the right section. The next three hours flew by as she stayed busy at the till or helped Gretchen serve at the Café. But in the back of her mind was the question, if Zane was out investigating on his own, who had his back?

Chapter 14 - Cracked

Gretchen turned the sign to CLOSED and locked the front door. She sighed tiredly and massaged her lower back before turning the front lights off.

"Business is getting better and better every day. I've put an ad in the paper for an assistant manager. I can't handle the baking and everything else too. I can't believe how obsessed everyone is with my muffins. It's almost as if they've got a little magic in them," she said with a smile.

Sarah grinned and shook her head as she finished sweeping the floor. She put the broom away and turned the lights off in the storeroom. "When will Zane be back do you think?"

Gretchen swished the worry away with her hand. "Oh don't worry about Zane Sarah. He'll show up when he shows up. He always does. In the meantime, let's head to the house and get dinner ready. I've got a pot roast in a crock pot with carrots and potatoes. I'm thinking peach cobbler for dessert. What do you say?" she said putting her arm around Sarah's waist.

Sarah grinned at Gretchen and relaxed. "That sounds amazing. And it's been forever since I've seen Agnes."

Gretchen let go of Sarah as they walked to the back of the store and out into the parking lot. "Well, she's changed quite a bit Sarah. Don't be upset when you see her and she doesn't recognize you," she warned.

Sarah nodded sadly and got into Gretchen's BMW. They drove the three blocks to Agnes' house which was on the outskirts of town. It was an older two story home with gables and white shutters. Sarah loved it.

Gretchen talked to Agnes's nurse for a few minutes, so Sarah took the opportunity to look through the front room. She walked slowly through the room, staring at the pictures covering the walls. She paused at a family picture and grinned when she saw Zane when he must have been maybe ten years old. Gretchen was standing behind Zane and his sisters next to a tall blond man who was grinning happily.

Gretchen came to stand beside her. "That's Bill. He died of a heart attack a few years ago. We found out his heart had a defect that no one ever knew about. He was a good man and he loved us," she said fondly with a hint of sadness in her voice.

Sarah could see now where Zane got his cheek bones and jaw structure from. "Was he a witch like you and Zane?" she asked curiously.

Gretchen shook her head and laughed. "No, Bill was as normal as they come. He knew I was a witch and that Zane was too. He didn't care though. He thought it was wonderful. He had a very open mind," she said wistfully.

Sarah frowned and followed Gretchen to the kitchen. "Wait, I thought Zane said witches aren't attracted to non-witches. He told me people are attracted to witches like moths are to porch lights but that porch lights aren't attracted to the moths."

Gretchen looked back and grinned at Sarah. "Well, when I was in college and saw Bill for the first time, I knew this Porch light was a goner. He was a life guard at the beach and when I saw his six pack abs I couldn't care less if he was a witch or an alien from another planet. He was mine," she said with gleeful satisfaction.

Sarah grinned delightedly at hearing Gretchen's love story. "So Zane was just making it all up then, huh?"

Gretchen frowned and shook her head. "Well, he's different than me. I'm just an average witch. I've never had to deal with the energy or the power that he has to deal with. You're the first girl he's ever wanted to be serious with that's for sure. Girls would come by the house and call him constantly but he always kept them at arm's length. And then he meets you and you're like him and he's a goner. Zane could never imagine himself being with someone who's normal. He's always been very aware of his power and I think to him a non-witch was never an option. So for him, I think the porch light analogy fits."

Sarah hummed in her throat but didn't say anything. She wondered if she could ever truly be attracted to someone who wasn't like she was and immediately thought of Lash. Lash wasn't a witch, but he emitted a dark charisma that was strangely compelling to her.

"Who's here?"

Sarah and Gretchen turned around together to see Agnes standing in the doorway looking suspicious. "Who are you and why are you in my house?" she demanded in a fierce voice.

Gretchen walked over and bent down to look into her mother's eyes. "It's me, mom. Gretchen. I'm just going to get dinner on the table and we can eat soon, okay? I brought you a friend to talk to. This is Sarah Hudson."

Agnes looked around Gretchen's shoulder and squinted at Sarah. "Oh I know little Sarah."

Gretchen turned around to stare at Sarah in shock. "She doesn't know me, but she knows you?" she asked in consternation.

Sarah shrugged uncomfortably and walked closer to Agnes. "Hi Mrs. Adams. I haven't seen you in a while. How are you doing?" she asked reaching out to take her hand.

Agnes looked up into Sarah's face and frowned. "Oh you've got to run faster Sarah. You've got to run faster than you've ever run before. If he catches you he'll never let you go. *Never*."

Sarah's mouth opened in shock and she blinked before turning to see an identical expression on Gretchen's face.

"She um, has moments of clarity sometimes, but this is, . . . this is something else," Gretchen said hesitantly.

Agnes took hold of Sarah's hand and pulled on her. "Come sit down and talk to me child. My legs are worn out from all the exercises that nurse makes me do. I feel like I've run a marathon. That lady there will make us dinner soon enough. Sometimes it tastes good and sometimes I might as well be eating saw dust but I'll make sure you leave fed tonight."

Sarah grinned at Gretchen's offended expression but had no choice but to follow Agnes to the couch.

Sarah sat down and Agnes plopped down next to her a little too close for comfort. Sarah looked closely at Agnes and noticed the changes that had taken place in the two months since she'd seen her. Agnes was in her mid-sixties and had always been very stylish with long salt and pepper hair that's she'd worn long and down to the middle of her back. She tended to wear sweater sets and plenty of jewelry. But now, Agnes was wearing a sweat suit and although of the finest quality and quite attractive, it just wasn't the Agnes she was used to. Her makeup was bare to nothing and her eyes seemed dimmer as if a light had gone out. That was the saddest part.

She felt a great sadness well up in her heart and she reached out and laid her hand over Agnes's. "Oh Agnes. Who did this to you?" she whispered under her breath.

Agnes gasped and laid her own hand over Sarah's. "That feels so strange," she said, looking up into Sarah's eyes.

Sarah looked back down at their hands and didn't see anything strange about it, but she started to feel a light warming where their hands were connected. Sarah looked up into Agnes' face. "Who hurt you Agnes? Who took your memories?" she asked softly.

Agnes looked confused and shook her head back and forth. "The light won't come. I can't find it anymore."

Sarah felt the warmth grow and studied their hands. She had healed people before. Maybe it was worth a try. She laid her other hand on the side of Agnes's head and leaned in close, closing her eyes. She sent her energy out to Agnes and surrounded her and felt Agnes's agitation seep away and a calm take over. She moved the energy deeper and moved in towards Agnes's mind. She didn't know what to do next, but went on instinct and opened her senses for anything that seemed off or out of place.

Sarah emptied everything out of her own mind and focused everything on Agnes and said clearly and firmly, "Come back Agnes. Come back now."

Agnes moaned loudly and leaned her head against Sarah's. The contact between their heads deepened the connection and Sarah felt a crack, like the crack in the window she'd made the other day. This crack was in Agnes's mind as if someone had tried to break her open. She felt around the crack and pushed against it slightly. Agnes whimpered.

"What is going on here?" Sarah heard Gretchen say as if from a great distance but ignored her. She sent more energy to the crack and tried to bring the edges together like she had Jill's neck. It felt different though, more like something had been removed. She focused on cells and the fragile connections in the tissues pulling and pulling with her power.

Agnes made a sighing sound and leaned more heavily against Sarah, almost pushing her off the couch. Sarah sent more soothing warmth towards Agnes's core and then gave everything she had to the crack.

What seemed like hours later, she felt herself come to the end of the crack and pulled away from Agnes. She still had her hands on Agnes so she felt the tremors run down her arms and into her torso.

She watched as Agnes slowly opened her eyes and blinked over and over again, bringing her face into focus. "Sarah Hudson. What are you doing here? If Race finds out I've contacted you he'll never forgive me," she said in a rush of words.

Sarah frowned and let her hands drop from Agnes as she pulled back. It hadn't worked. Her mind was still gone.

Gretchen walked slowly towards her mother and knelt down beside her, resting her head on her knees. "Oh Mom. If only it had worked," she said, her voice shaking with unshed tears.

Agnes laid her hand on Gretchen's hair and caressed her daughter's head. "Gretchen, what are you doing here sweetie? I thought you and Zane were coming for Christmas? Is everything okay?"

Gretchen slowly lifted her head, tears swimming in her eyes as she stared up in to her mother's face. She lifted a hand to Agnes' cheek and cleared her throat before talking. "*Mom?*"

Agnes laughed and leaned down to hug her daughter. "Of course it's me. Who'd you think I was, Marilyn Monroe? Now come sit down and catch me up on everything. Where's Zane? What's that boy been up to?" she said patting the couch seat beside her.

Sarah and Gretchen exchanged hopeful looks and Sarah stood up. "I'll just go set the table," she murmured as Gretchen rose up to sit on the couch, throwing her arms around her mother's shoulders and laughing softly.

She walked out of the room wondering for the millionth time what it would have been like to have the love of a mother.

She puttered around the kitchen for fifteen minutes, looking through cabinets until she found what she was looking for. She opened the lid to the crock pot and snagged a few carrots while she waited for either Zane to show up or for Gretchen and Agnes to come into the kitchen. As she munched on the carrots, she reached out with her mind for Zane. She couldn't wait to tell him about Agnes. He'd be so excited to find out that his grandmother remembered him and his mother now.

She reached out with her mind, not knowing at what distance she could find him, but not having anything better to do than to try. She sent pulses of energy out searching for the warmth that was solely Zane's. She turned in all directions searching for some answering pulse of energy but met with nothing. She walked over to the window and looked out into the dark sky and tried one more time. She knew he was out there and she knew what he was doing was dangerous. Maybe he was just too busy to answer back? Or too far out?

She shrugged with a frown and looked at the crock pot again. She felt like she was starving to death. If she didn't have some of that roast soon, she was going to pass out from hunger.

She sat down and tapped her fingers on the table lazily as Gretchen walked into the kitchen followed by her mother. Sarah slowly stood up, looking questioningly at Gretchen.

"Sarah, my mom seems to remember everything up until three months ago. About a month before Zane and I moved here."

Agnes moved around her daughter and came to stand in front of Sarah, looking worried. "Child, you shouldn't be here. If Race finds out I've made contact with you there'll be hell to pay."

Sarah frowned and felt angry all of a sudden. "Why wouldn't Race want you to talk to me?" she demanded, looking at Gretchen and seeing her look just as perplexed.

"Because he doesn't want you to know you're a witch. He wants you to be safe. If anything were to happen to you like it what happened to Rachel, he would never forgive himself," she muttered and sat down rubbing her head as if she had a head ache.

Sarah exchanged worried glances with Gretchen. "Okay Agnes, I'll go. I was just here to say hi to Zane. I'm glad you're feeling better," she said and then looked towards the pot roast yearningly.

Gretchen looked at her helplessly but nodded. She walked her to the front door and then put her arms around Sarah, hugging her tightly. "Thank you Sarah. Thank you so much. I knew there was a way to bring her back, I just didn't know how. She's tired and needs to rest now, but we'll figure it all out. We'll talk tomorrow okay?" she said, and opened the door for her, eager to get back to her mother.

Sarah nodded and smiled over her shoulder as she walked out onto the front porch. "No problem Gretchen. I'm just happy I could do something."

Gretchen nodded, her eyes filling with tears as she turned back towards her mom.

Sarah stared at the closed door and sighed, feeling so empty, hungry and exhausted that she wasn't sure she could walk the two blocks to the store. She shoved her hands into the front pockets of her jeans and walked down the steps and onto the side walk. She made her way slowly home and used the key Gretchen had given her to let herself in to the store.

She grabbed a water bottle and a left over muffin and trudged up the stairs. She locked her apartment door and leaned against the wall by her little window as she devoured the muffin and drank her water. She stared at the dark night and felt suddenly very cold. She frowned at the unfriendly sky and shut her blinds blocking out the outside world.

She didn't even bother to find her pajamas and just crawled under her covers with her jeans and t-shirt and immediately fell asleep. She slept so soundly, it was only the pounding on her bedroom door that woke her the next morning.

She moaned as she threw the covers off, wondering why her body ached and felt sore. She stumbled to the door and barely remembered to say, "Who is it?"

"It's Gretchen, Sarah."

Sarah immediately opened the door and let Gretchen in on a wave of floral scent, a whirl of her silk gray skirt and restless energy. Sarah winced at the light Gretchen brought in with her and stumbled back to bed, laying her heavy head back onto her pillow.

"How's Agnes?" she croaked, closing her eyes.

Gretchen looked around her room, walking quickly to the bathroom and peeking inside. She then walked to the closet and opened the doors, pulling the clothes from the very back towards the front.

"Zane!" she called out, looking suspiciously at the underside of the bed.

Sarah looked at her as if she had completely lost it. "Gretchen, are you okay?" she asked tiredly.

Gretchen ran her hands through her hair and looked even more agitated. "Zane never came home last night. I was thinking that possibly he was here with you."

Sarah raised her eyebrows at the insinuation and felt a wave of embarrassment wash over her at the implication. "Uh, *no*. We just met Monday, remember? I like your son a lot, but um, we wouldn't spend the night together," she said, feeling a warm blush washed up her neck and over her cheeks.

Gretchen winced and nodded. "Then he's in trouble Sarah. Hurry and get dressed and come downstairs. We've got to do something."

As what Gretchen said sank in, Sarah felt a cold and dark fear slip into her heart. She quickly changed and pulled her hair up into a messy pony tail. She ran down the stairs and pushed through the door and walked into the store.

"Gretchen!" she called moving towards the front of the store and came face to face with Agnes Adams. "*Oh*," she said coming to a standstill.

Agnes looked her up and down and smiled kindly at her. "No worries Sarah, Gretchen brought me up to speed. We'll talk about your father later. Right now, let's focus on Zane."

Sarah nodded her head quickly in agreement and moved around Agnes to walk quickly to the front of the store where Gretchen was at the till, talking hurriedly on her cell phone.

"Zane, call me right now. *Please* Zane. Call me. I'm worried," she said and then lowered her cell phone to the counter staring at it as if it had betrayed her.

Sarah grasped Gretchen's hand in hers and then wished she hadn't as all of Gretchen's emotions poured into her. Feelings of worry, despair and agitation felt like acid tripping along her nerve endings and she had to let go.

"Gretchen, where did he go yesterday? Did he tell you where he was going?"

Gretchen looked up and met her eyes uncertainly. "He told me he was going back to your dad's house. He wanted to know what happened between Race and your mom. He wanted to know why Race hasn't been a father to you."

Sarah felt her heart twist and she turned away. "I'm going to look for him," she said and walked towards the front door.

Gretchen lifted her hand. "That's too dangerous Sarah. You know Zane wouldn't want you to put yourself in danger. There are people who would love to have your power under their control. We don't know what we're up against here."

Sarah shook her head impatiently. "I'm more than capable of taking care of myself Gretchen. I just about fried your son yesterday and that was only because I was irritated. Besides, maybe Zane is totally fine. Maybe he's still investigating something and lost track of time," she said, the doubt leaching through her voice.

Gretchen sighed and opened the door for Sarah. "Bring him home Sarah. Bring him home."

Agnes reached out and touched her arm before she disappeared. "He's in trouble. He's hurt. I can tell. You need to hurry."

Sarah winced and rushed outside and then stopped immediately when she realized she didn't know where to go. If only Zane had opened up to her about his plans yesterday. She glanced down the street and then looked down the other side. She closed her eyes and pushed out with her energy. She pushed and pushed but came up with nothing. She lowered her head to try harder when her cell phone vibrated in her pocket. She fished it out and stared at the

119

screen. She growled in irritation at the interruption and then gasped as she saw the subject line. ZANE

She opened the text. Your boyfriend is with us. Want to see him?

Sarah's eyes widened in horror and she turned to walk back into the store, pushing the door open with her hip as she texted back. Yes! Where is he?

"Sarah?" Gretchen called from the back of the store.

Sarah ignored her and Agnes as they came to stand next to her. She stared intently at the screen and waited for the vibration to come. Seconds later it came. Meet us at Drake's house. 1123 South 400 East. Hurry.

Sarah showed the texts to Gretchen and swallowed thickly, feeling as if she could throw up.

"We should go to the police. They've kidnapped him. They've hurt him, I just know it. They've crossed the line."

Gretchen nodded her head. "Give me your phone and I'll drive over to the police station with Agnes to show them this proof. You head over to Drake's house and see what you can do," she said, her eyes looking steel gray and mean.

Sarah nodded her head knowing that if they'd hurt Zane, she would use all the energy she had on them.

Chapter 15 - Just Say No

Sarah glanced at the address one more time and then turned and ran out the door. She pushed her energy into her legs as she ran as fast as she could towards the address in her mind. It was in the neglected part of town. The oldest part. She flew past buildings and shops, her arms swinging faster and faster as her legs pumped in a whirl of movement. She rounded a corner and came to a jog as she caught sight of the house across the street.

She slowed to a walk and studied the small bungalow. It was light yellow with black shutters and a black roof. The bright red door was cheery and welcoming in a foul way that reminded her of Hansel and Gretel. But in this story, the witch was the one in trouble. She stepped across the street and as she came closer she could feel the darkness reach out to embrace her. She immediately flung her energy up as a protection but some of the coldness seeped in and around her chest, making her scared for what Zane had been experiencing all night long.

She crossed the street and walked over to the house next door instead of running to Drake's house. She pretended to knock on the door as she turned her head and studied the house. It was small and cozy looking. It didn't look like a psychopath lived there at all.

Nobody was peeking out the windows that she could see. They probably hadn't expected her to make it to the house that fast. If they were smart, they'd be watching for her. She glanced towards the back of the house and noticed a small basement window with a light on. She walked over to the edge of the porch and jumped over, landing on her feet. She walked quickly to the fence between the houses and vaulted over easily. She stayed close to the side of the house, ignoring the cold darkness and crouched down to peek into the window. She didn't see anything but bare concrete floors at first. But then she saw a form crumpled in the corner and felt her heart stutter and beat faster.

Zane! she called out with her mind.

Silence

Sarah sent her energy out of herself and towards the crumpled figure, enveloping the body with all the warmth and energy she had to give. The form shuddered and moved slightly. She heard a door slam somewhere in the house and straightened up. She felt rage pour through her at what her aunt Lena and Drake were willing to do to use her. They had hurt Zane and they were going to pay.

She glanced down at the crumpled form still huddled in the corner and tried one last time.

Zane! she called out with her mind again.

Saaaaarr, she heard as a very faint whisper that barely touched the edges of her mind.

Sarah swallowed her panic and turned to sprint around the house. She bounded up the front steps and pounded loudly on the front door with both fists.

"Lena!" she screamed as loud as she could, her energy rushing through her blood stream like a train.

"Lena!" she screamed again and kicked the door over and over again, denting the metal and scratching the red paint.

The door opened slowly and carefully revealing Drake standing before her, smiling exultantly.

"We knew you'd come. When Lena told me about how willing you and your mother were to throw your sorry lives away for men, I knew our only chance with you would be using the boy. Sorry it had to come to this Sarah, but you left us no choice. Come in my dear, come in.

If you only knew how long I've been waiting for this," Drake said with a grin and a swagger as he opened the door wide for her to walk past.

Sarah felt her rage build higher and higher and her energy flash down her back and through her fingers.

She calmed her expression and walked through the doors but then shocked them both when she threw herself on Drake, grabbing his neck and sending waves of energy through her hands into his body.

His cocky expression faded to horror as his body started to shake and he started drooling.

"Let him go Sarah or you'll never see your boyfriend alive again. I'm prepared to do whatever it takes to get your cooperation Sarah. *Let him go!*" Lena screamed.

Sarah dropped Drake and turned to her aunt who smiled cruelly at her. "I knew you'd do anything for a boy. The first cute boy to smile at you and you give up the chance of a life time. You'd do anything for him, wouldn't you? You're so like your mom you make me sick. Now, do everything I tell you and I'll make sure your boyfriend gets home safe and sound. If you refuse? Then his fate is on your head."

Sarah felt a new rush of power rip through her body and felt more than heard the light bulbs explode throughout the hallway and family room.

Lena winced and turned to look at the shattered glass across the floor. She looked uncertain for a moment and then looked to Drake for help, but he was huddled on the floor whimpering and twitching uncontrollably.

"Do that again and I'll make sure the boy is missing a few fingers before he comes back."

Sarah ground her teeth and thought of her aunt hurting Zane and shuddered. "Just for the record, you're the one throwing your life away over a man. Not me. Do you really think you're above the law Lena? Last time I checked, kidnapping and torture were enough to get you thrown in jail for a few decades."

Lena glared at her and put her hands on her hips. "As soon as the ceremony is done, I'll be gone and you'll never see me again. They won't be able to find us. Drake has already made plans for us. We're leaving within the hour."

Sarah felt Zane whisper something in her mind, but it was too faint to understand. She couldn't waste any more time.

She looked at her aunt sadly but then gathered her energy and sent it shooting out towards her aunt, letting it shatter against her chest.

Lena flew back as if she'd been hit by a car, gasping and looking surprised for a moment before closing her eyes and collapsing onto the floor. Lena lay twitching on the ground, unconscious, pale and immobile.

Sarah stared at the two bodies lying on either side of her and felt the TV screen explode in the next room followed by all the glasses in the kitchen. The noise was deafening and violent. The front windows cracked in a cacophony of sound that had her jumping. She looked frantically around and hurried down the hallway looking for the basement entrance.

She found it next to the kitchen and ran down the stairs as fast as she could move. The light bulb overhead exploded immediately as she rushed by leaving only the light from the windows to guide her.

She jumped down the last two steps and flew to the corner she had seen from the window. The form lying under the blanket moved suddenly and a woman sat up, grinning at her and holding a gun.

"We knew you'd try to pull something," she said and stood up slowly as if her knees hurt.

Sarah gasped in shock and surprise, looking around as she felt a presence move behind her. She turned and saw the other woman who was a regular at her aunt's meetings.

"Looks like it's just you and me, Venus," the woman said, also holding a gun on Sarah.

"Yeah, Lena thought Drake needed back up. Looks like they both did. But we're not playing around anymore Sarah. I'm more than happy to shoot you right now if you don't put your hands behind your head and walk right back up those stairs. We're getting in a van and going for a little drive. Forget Drake and Lena. We can do the ceremony ourselves," she said in a high excited voice looking over Sarah's shoulder at Venus.

Venus gasped in pleasure. "I would love that Delilah. Drake always got on my nerves anyways and Lena's just a fool. The only good she's ever done was tell us about her niece. Come on. Move it," she ordered pushing the gun against Sarah's head, bruising her and moving her back towards the stairs.

Sarah glanced quickly around the basement but didn't feel any other people there. *Where was Zane?* she wondered. She didn't want to hurt any more people until she knew where he was. She needed answers.

"So, if Zane isn't here, where is he?" she asked as she walked slowly up the stairs, hating the crunching sound of the fragile glass under her shoes.

The woman named Venus pushed her with her hand, making her stumble and fall on the stairs. The glass covering the old wooden steps immediately sliced her hands and she cried out in pain.

"Don't worry about him. He's fine. You're the only one we're interested in."

Sarah slowly stood up, feeling pain tear up her nerve endings, making the power stretch and snap within her. If she didn't find a release for all the power whipping through her system soon, she honestly didn't know what would happen. She felt like she might disintegrate. Her hair was coiling tighter and the t-shirt she was wearing was starting to fade in color as the electricity was almost burning it. She reached down to wipe some of the blood off her hands and felt the glass that had been imbedded in her hands fall out. She stared down at her bloody hands and saw the cuts and lacerations had already started to heal.

The woman Delilah opened the basement door into the kitchen and walked quickly through the hallway and into the family room where she stopped in shock as she saw Drake and Lena still prone on the floor, their chins covered with spit and strange red spots all over their faces. Lena's eyes were closed, but Drakes' were wide open staring at the ceiling as he continued to twitch.

"Venus! Look at them. *What did you do*?" Delilah asked, stepping back from Sarah and raising her gun, with hands that were now shaking.

Venus rushed to Lena's side and felt for a pulse. "She's alive and breathing. What kind of girl would hurt her own aunt?" she asked in disgust raising her gun to point at Sarah's head too.

Sarah felt the power literally dripping off her fingers as she started to shake. "What kind of aunt would want to hurt her niece is the real question?"

Delilah lifted her head and sneered at her. "You should be grateful for all Lena's done for you throughout the years. She's given you a home to live in and all she asked in return was a little blood, hair and a few words. We should kill you right now," she said, her finger shaking on the gun.

Sarah closed her eyes to send all the energy from her body out at the same time. She'd have to send it in two different directions at once, or she'd be dead. She'd never attempted anything like it before and didn't even know if it was possible.

"Delilah *no*! If you kill her, she's useless. She has to say the words willingly or it won't work. She can't speak if she's not breathing."

Delilah lowered her gun slightly as she looked at Venus. "But . . . .,"

She never finished her sentence. Her words died as a man walked up behind her and grabbed her by the throat.

"Put the guns down both of you right now," he said, his voice gravelly and old sounding.

She felt Venus jump to the side as she lifted her gun to get a good shot at the intruder.

The man held up his hand and Venus crumpled as her foot left the ground. The gun fell uselessly to the ground, leaving silence except for Delilah's gasps of breath.

"Please. Please let me go," she begged, clawing at the man's hands grasping her neck tightly.

Sarah moved slowly back from the pair, until a wall met her back. She stared at the man and knew immediately who it was. Race Livingston. He looked at her and met her gaze with the same green eyes she had. Race glanced at the back of Delilah's head and she crumpled without him even moving his hand or saying anything. He let go and ended up with her gun in his hand before her body could even hit the floor, landing right next to Drake's body.

Sarah groaned and covered her face with her hands. "I wasn't able to find out where Zane is! I was going to try and get information out of them, but you've ruined it," she said accusingly flexing her fingers.

Race looked irritated for a second and then looked away. "They lied then."

Sarah clasped her shaking arms around her middle and glared at the man who might be her father. "Yeah, shocking. Now what are we going to do? Did you kill them?"

Race leaned over Delilah and picked her up as if she were a rag doll. She weighed at least 170 pounds. He whispered something low and rusty into the woman's face and her eyes popped open eerily.

"Where's the boy? Where is Zane Miner?" he demanded as her eyes opened unnaturally wide.

Delilah whimpered and tried to speak. Race whispered another word and the woman contorted in pain, gasping and crying out for him to stop. Sarah grimaced in disgust and eased away from the wall just in case she could hear something of value

"I'll give you one more chance and then this young girl here is going to turn you into a vegetable. She's about to explode with energy. Better you than me. Where is the boy?" he asked, shaking her this time, making her head snap back and forth. She raised her head and looked at Race and whispered a word. "*Forest.*"

Sarah heard the whispered word and ran past Race and the woman and out the door and down the stairs. Race appeared in the doorway and shouted after her to stop.

"The forest is too big Sarah! You'll never find him this way!" he shouted, sounding fainter and fainter as she left the little yellow house far behind. She ran the half a block to the edge of the forest.

The little town they lived in wrapped around the forests and there were three main access points. She let her power take over and went faster and faster until she felt like she was flying. She entered the walking path that was the East entrance to the forest and then let herself go like she never had before. She sent her energy out in a net in all directions and called out Zane's name over and over inside her mind.

She ran past markers and trail signs ignoring everything and jumping and ducking automatically when she needed too.

Zane! she screamed in her mind and paused, gasping for air as she felt her name echo back to her, resonating in her chest.

Sarah.

He was near. She leaned over panting and closed her eyes. *I'm here Zane. I'm in the forest. Help me find you,* she begged.

Dark, wet. Feel my heart. Feel my heart, Zane whispered back to her.

Sarah stood up and closed her eyes and lifted her arms as she turned slowly in a circle, sending her power out again. The energy flowed from her fingers and flew from her hair. Her head twisted to the right as she felt a pulse of warmth answer her. She drank in a deep breath and leapt through the leaves and twigs and rocks and went deeper and deeper into the forest. She broke through five minutes later in to a clearing where someone had built a primitive hut. She knew this time that Zane was inside.

The woman standing in front of the hut, holding a rifle was the last woman from her aunt's meetings. She looked half hysterical and more than slightly demented. Her arms were shaking and she was sweating profusely. Sarah knew instinctively that this woman was far more dangerous than the other four. This woman wanted to shoot her.

"Why are *you* here? You're supposed to be dead now. Where is everyone?" she demanded, walking slowly towards Sarah.

Sarah lifted her hands in surrender and stayed where she was. If she could get the woman to lower the gun or point it somewhere other than her, she'd send out energy and have her on the ground. But the gun was pointed right at her heart and her trigger finger looked slippery.

Sarah swallowed, feeling her adrenaline weep through her blood. "They're done. All four of them are lying on the floor where I left them. The plan is a failure. It's all over. Just put the gun down and I'll tell the police that you tried to help me. Just put it down," she said in a soothing voice that sounded deep and unlike hers.

The woman shook her head quickly back and forth. "I just wanted out, you know. They told me my life would be better. I wouldn't have to work cleaning houses anymore. We were going to be rich Drake said."

Sarah grasped onto that thought. "I've got money. I'll give you everything I have if you'll put the rifle down."

The woman tripped on a rock and almost went down but righted herself quickly and pointed the rifle at Sarah's head, looking fiercer because of her embarrassment.

"How much you got?" she demanded, looking over her shoulder at the shack.

Sarah lied and said, "I have about twelve thousand dollars left from my mother's life insurance policy. I'll wire it into your bank account today if you'll put the gun down and promise not to hurt me or that boy in there."

The woman laughed and wiped her nose on her sleeve. "He's not hurt. He's just drugged. Okay, you got a deal. I'll take the money. I'm getting out of here. Forget this crap. I'm gone," she said almost in relief and lowered the gun so the muzzle was pointed straight into the dirt.

Sarah lowered her arms and smiled in gratitude at the woman and then sent so much energy careening towards her she was knocked seven feet back, hitting her back and head on a tree. She collapsed silently in a heap as Sarah rushed past her to the shack, stepping in through the dark entrance and crouching down by Zane's side.

"Zane!" she whispered, crying as she saw his bound hands and feet. She touched the zip ties digging into his skin and they burst open, looking melted. She turned him onto his back and pushed his hair away from his eyes.

He wasn't breathing right. He was breathing very shallow. She laid her head on his chest and felt his heartbeat. It was there, but it felt very weak.

She lifted her head in panic and looked around, not knowing what to do. Gretchen had taken her phone and she couldn't carry him. She paused in her frantic thought patterns and lowered her head to his. If it worked for Agnes, maybe she could heal Zane. She lay down beside Zane and wrapped her arms and legs around him, touching him everywhere she could. She closed her eyes and used all of the power rushing through her body and changed it into a healing flow of power and sent it into Zane's body, wrapping around him and then moving inside of him.

She could feel the drugs they'd given him everywhere in his system. She let her power take over and felt the toxins and chemicals start to seep out of Zane's pores as she urged her power to cleanse his blood. She could feel his heart beat a little stronger a few minutes later. Her clothes started to feel damp as she forced Zane to sweat and purge his body of the poisons.

Sarah felt herself weaken as all of her excess energy was almost gone. Zane made a noise and moved his arm. She opened her eyes and lifted her head up and away from Zane so she could get up and kneel over him. She pushed her hair behind her ears and leaned down to touch his face.

"Zane, can you hear me?" she asked softly, kissing his brow and his cheeks.

"Sarah?" Zane said, his eyes still closed and his voice weak and broken.

"Yes, it's me. We've got to get you out of here," she said, rubbing her hands down his arms, feeling the moisture through his shirt.

Zane moaned and began retching as if he would throw up. Sarah grabbed his shoulders and tried to turn him as he gagged and shuddered.

"It's okay Zane. It's going to be okay," she promised over and over again, feeling his sickness inside of her.

Zane's retching finally subsided and he fell back onto the rough blanket, exhausted. "I knew you would come Sarah. I could hear you calling for me," he whispered, trying to focus on her face.

Sarah's face crumpled and she began to cry helplessly. "How am I going to get you out of here?" she sobbed knowing how weak he was.

"Just lay here beside me for a moment. I need your warmth," he said.

Sarah nodded her head and wiped her eyes. She lifted Zane's head and slipped her arm underneath him, lying chest to chest with him. She closed her eyes and held him close, sending the rest of her waning power into his body, filling him with as much strength as she could give him. They lay like that for at least fifteen minutes, not saying anything, just breathing and listening to each other's heart beats.

"Your system is still overloaded with drugs. I can't seem to get it all out," Sarah whispered against his hair.

Zane moved his arm as if to comfort her. "You saved my life. I thought I was going to die Sarah. If you hadn't gotten here in time, my heart would have given out."

Sarah felt her body shake at the thought but didn't say anything. "Did they take your cell phone?" she asked, already knowing they had

Zane nodded. "But you're welcome to check for yourself," he said in a faintly teasing voice that had her smiling.

She eased carefully away from Zane, sitting up and grinning. "Why am I being so slow? That woman has to have one. She has to."

Sarah jumped up and rushed out of the shack and towards the woman still lying prone on the forest floor. Sarah pushed her over with her foot and then patted her down looking for a phone. She found it in a side pocket of her cargo pants. She ran back to the shack and kneeled down by Zane who was now able to open his eyes even though he still looked white as sheet.

"What's your mom's number?"

Zane told her and she dialed the number, pounding her fist on her knee as she waited. On the third ring Gretchen answered, yelling Zane's name. *"Zane!"*

"No Gretchen, it's me. But I've found him. He's too weak to move though. We need help getting him out of here. We're in the forest about two miles towards the center. Start off of Coleman Road and go about a mile and a half and then take a sharp right until you come to a clearing. You'll need a four wheeler or something. The terrain is kind of rough and it's no place for a car. And Gretchen, he's going to need to go straight to the hospital. They drugged him."

She talked to Gretchen for a few more minutes and then held the phone up to Zane's ear so he could say hi to his mom. But pulled it away seconds later. "Hurry! You can talk later. He needs help now," she ordered and then disconnected.

Zane smiled faintly back up at her. "You're kind of feisty, aren't you?"

Sarah threw the phone away and lay down by Zane again, wrapping him in her power and heat.

"You have no idea," she said darkly.

Zane's hand came up to touch her hair and she sighed in relief, as her body finally started to let down. Zane would be safe now. Zane would be okay.

"I was supposed to save you. What are you doing saving me?" he said in a disappointed voice.

Sarah smiled and looked up into his eyes. "That's so sexist. Really, the only reason I bothered was because it's Flirt All You Want Friday. I didn't want you thinking you could skip out on such an important day," she said trying to smile and then ruined it by crying on him.

Zane's eyes turned soft and he reached a shaky finger up to touch one of her tears. "Out of all the days to be kidnapped I had to pick a Friday. I hope you'll forgive me and let me make it up to you next week."

Sarah sniffed and hugged him hard, knowing she was lucky to even have another week with him.

"So how did they get to you?" she asked curiously.

Zane frowned and closed his eyes. "I was planning on going back to Race's house but I had a feeling Drake was more of a danger to you. So I broke in and found his journal Sarah. I was so caught up in reading his plans for you that I didn't hear him come in. He came up behind me and stuck a syringe in my back. From what I was reading, I'm positive that syringe was meant for you. Before I passed out, your aunt came in and when Drake told her who I was, she kicked me in the side. That's when I passed out. I'm so sorry Sarah. I let you down."

Sarah reached up and yanked on his hair. "Don't be an idiot. You could be the most powerful witch in the world, but if someone gets the drop on you and drugs you, you're going to go down for the count."

Zane sighed unhappily. "Still, not the way I had planned things going," he muttered.

Sarah smiled and held him closer. "You feel stronger already," she said in surprise.

Zane nodded his head, drawing shapes on her throat. "You do that to me. You make me stronger. Give me another half hour and I might actually be able to stand up. Heck, give me a couple hours and Flirting Friday is back on schedule."

Sarah laughed, knowing he was definitely feeling better if he could think about flirting with her. She was so tired, but she wrapped her arms around him again, willing more toxins out of his blood. Fifteen minutes later, the sound of high powered motors roaring through the forest had her pulling away from him and standing up.

"The cavalry has arrived," she said in relief and walked out to greet Gretchen and three police officers on four wheelers.

Gretchen screamed and then fainted as she stared at Sarah's hands. Sarah looked down in confusion and then realized all of the blood from the glass was still on her hands. Her pants made it look like she was an extra from a haunted house.

The officer with Gretchen ran to her side and started checking her out as he barked questions at her in a rapid fire succession. As Sarah tried the best she could to tell him what happened, the other officers focused on Zane and the fallen woman.

Sarah kneeled down as if to pat Gretchen's shoulder, but sent a zap of energy through her system instead. She whispered the word, *awake*, and watched in relief as Gretchen's eyes fluttered open. "You're missing the grand reunion Gretchen. Zane's in there," she said pointed at the shack.

Gretchen reached up and felt her head as if it were sore but then rolled to her side and stood up, weaving back and forth a little before hurrying to the shack.

Two police officers worked on carrying Zane out of the shack, while the third officer handcuffed the still unconscious woman. They put Zane on a stretcher and placed him on the trailer hooked to one of the four wheelers.

After kissing Zane's forehead and touching his cheek one last time Gretchen grabbed Sarah in her arms and held her so tightly she thought she was going to pass out.

"You saved him Sarah. He said he was dying and you saved him. Bless you, bless you."

Sarah looked nervously at the police officers who were trying to get the woman to wake up. She whispered into Gretchen's ear. "How am I going to explain what I did to that woman and to my aunt and Drake?"

Gretchen slipped a Taser from her pocket into Sarah's hands. "Race told me I should give this to you. Just tell them that you tasered them and leave the rest to me."

Zane was taken to the hospital in the city while she and Gretchen went to the police station with the police officers.

Chapter 16 - Duality

After two hours of speaking with a police woman they'd brought in to question her, Sarah left the station with Gretchen. She was so worn out she didn't know if she could move.

"Honey, I'm getting us a pizza and then you're going to bed. Everything you've been through today and what you did to save Zane has worn you out," she said, looking guilty and relieved at the same time.

"I don't even know if I have the strength to eat Gretchen. Forcing the toxins out of Zane's blood drained me of everything. I want to go see Zane in the hospital though," she said and then yawned, leaning her head back against the smooth leather of Gretchen's BMW.

Gretchen patted her knee and pulled up in front of the shop. "Here's the plan. You're about to collapse. You've got to eat something though, so eat a muffin and then get at least ten hours of sleep. I'll have my mom come open the store in the morning and then we'll see about getting you to the hospital. Okay?"

Sarah closed her eyes and nodded. She didn't have the strength to argue. Gretchen pulled her out of the car and with an arm around her shoulders helped her in the door and up the stairs. As Sarah lay on the bed, Gretchen pulled her shoes off and then disappeared for a moment, reappearing a couple minutes later with a muffin and a Dr. Pepper.

"Can you at least take a bite Sarah?" Gretchen urged, leaning over her.

Sarah mumbled something and turned over, her eyelids closing against her will.

She woke up the next day with the sun shining brightly through her windows. She turned over and saw a vase of flowers on her night stand that hadn't been there the day before. She smiled at the kindness and then squeaked when she saw what time it was. 1:00pm.

Sarah pulled her still lethargic body out of bed and hopped in the shower, turning the water to as hot as she could stand it. She finished and then with a towel wrapped around herself, scanned her closet. She chose aquamarine jeans with a plain white t-shirt and her tennis shoes. She thought about seeing Zane at the hospital and took an extra two minutes to cover the circles under her eyes and put on lip gloss and mascara.

She walked down and into the store, looking quickly around for Gretchen.

"She just went back to the hospital Sarah. She said if you ever woke up to tell you that she'd be back at 4," Agnes said as she finished dusting the moldings above the door.

Sarah frowned and felt like kicking something. "I can't believe I slept so long. I've never done that before."

"Well, you've never given everything you had to give before either. I checked on you this morning and your aura is still faded. You gave a little too much and now you're weak. You still need to rest and more than anything, you need to eat something. I have orders to get you anything you want. I'm closing the store for lunch and I'm taking you to Fernando's. That man can grill a steak like no other. You a vegetarian?"

Sarah grinned and shook her head. "Nah, a steak sounds great."

Agnes locked the shop up and they walked two streets over to the busy restaurant. Agnes chatted about the changes to the store and sounded irritated. "Gretchen's here for a couple months and now we're selling gourmet muffins and artwork."

Sarah smiled down at Agnes's grouchy face. "Well, how has business been?"

Agnes huffed out more irritation. "It looks like sales have increased 27%. She might know what she's doing there. But she should have asked me first."

Sarah rolled her eyes at the illogical reasoning behind this and let it go. They walked into the warm and fragrant restaurant and Sarah's mouth instantly started to water. Agnes held up two fingers and they were seated by the window, facing the street.

"We'll have two steaks, the best you got, two house salads, some potato salad and milk shakes," she told the waiter as he began to hand her the menu. He smiled, put the menus back under his arm and walked away to put the orders in.

"Now tell me everything. Gretchen only got what she heard you tell the police. What really happened to my boy?" Agnes asked, smearing enough butter for a loaf of bread on one slice of sour dough.

Sarah took a sip of her water and looked out the window. "It turns out I have two different gifts. I can heal and I can harm," she said, remembering Drake, her aunt and the women.

Agnes nodded. "That's usually the way it works. It's the duality of power. But it all comes down to the same thing, doesn't it? From the beginning of time, certain people have been blessed with more than others. That blessing of power comes from God and He expects us to use it to help, to heal and yes, to protect. You didn't hurt those people yesterday because you wanted to or because you enjoyed it or out of spite. You did what had to be done to save my grandson's life. There's nothing to be ashamed of," she said sternly.

Sarah nodded. "So you think our powers come from God. Most witches I've read about say their power is from Satan or the earth or weird goddesses."

Agnes snorted and motioned the waiter for more bread. "Why worship the earth and nature when God is the one who created it all? It's ridiculous. And those Satan worshippers who think he's going to share his power with them, they're just like that man and your aunt. Wanting something they shouldn't. Satan doesn't share. He destroys. No girl, you listen to me. Gretchen told me you insist on calling it psychokinesis. I don't care what you call it. I don't like the word witch myself to be honest. But you have a responsibility. If you take that seriously and do what you can to help others, you'll be just fine."

138

Sarah smiled and relaxed as what Agnes said clicked into place. "I like that."

Agnes grinned and then patted her hand. "Now tell me everything."

Sarah went through everything from the beginning to the end, but she had her own questions.

"Why didn't Gretchen call the police right after I left? Why did she call Race?" she asked grumpily.

Agnes opened her mouth to say something but was interrupted by their waiter bringing their food. The steaks were still sizzling and she forgot what she was saying as she focused all of her attention on the fuel in front of her. Agnes laughed heartily as Sarah consumed every bite on her plate and started eyeing Agnes's salad.

"Don't worry, here comes your chocolate milkshake. You're in for a treat," she said as the waiter placed the tall glasses, topped with whipped cream and a cherry in front of them.

Sarah closed her eyes and sighed in pleasure. "This was exactly what my body needed," she said in satisfaction as she grabbed the milk shake

"You're already looking perkier. Now, while you're slurping that down, I'll answer your question. Gretchen called Race because I insisted she did. She fought me on it. She was so worried and hysterical yesterday she would have called in the National Guard. But Race was the one to handle that situation. And from what you've told me, he did. Race is a strong witch and like you, he has certain gifts that come in handy from time to time."

Sarah studied Agnes over the top of her milkshake, frowning a little. "I just don't get it. I think you know more about me and my mom and Race than I do. What happened? And why, if Race is my father, did he let my crazy aunt raise me?" she demanded, wiping her mouth with her napkin and pushing the now empty glass away from her.

Agnes looked away from her and out the window. "I know your aunt told you your mother died of pancreatic cancer. She didn't. She died because she got caught in between Race and another witch. A witch that had turned bad. He had threatened to hurt you if Race didn't do what he wanted. And don't ask, because he's never shared the particulars with me. But Race had had enough and went after Charles. Oh, a witch fight isn't something you ever want to see. It's brutal and it's lethal most of the times. Charles had Race and was about to crack his scull in two when your mom came home and saw what was happening. She threw herself between the men and was killed instantly. Charles saw what he'd done and immediately disappeared. Unfortunately, your aunt was in the doorway, holding you and saw the whole thing. She was furious with Race and blamed him for your mother's death. She told him that she would tell everyone the truth about him if he didn't give you to her to raise. Oh, he could have taken you and left and raised you just fine, but he believed Lena. He was dying of grief and he thought it was his fault. He was too heart broken and guilty to be a good father anyways. So Lena took you." Agnes said and then paused to take a sip of water before continuing.

"A few years later when Race sobered up and started thinking clearly, he went back to Lena and told her he wanted you back. She laughed in his face. She told him he was a freak and that if he cared for you at all, he wouldn't want his daughter being raised by a witch. She promised him that she would raise you to be normal and that you would be safe. Race believed her and backed off. But then Lena got mixed up with a bad group and I started worrying about you. You'd come in after school, looking so miserable and shooting off so much energy I was just grateful nothing caught on fire most days. I approached Race about being your mentor and helping you with your abilities but by then, he was so bitter and angry at the world and life in general that he said no. He thought being a witch had ruined his life and ruined Rachel's life. He didn't want you to even know you were a witch. Race hated himself. He didn't want you to ever feel like that about yourself."

Sarah closed her eyes and leaned back against the chair, feeling full and lethargic and incredibly sad for her mother and father.

"But didn't he know Lena was trying to force me to be a witch? Why would she throw that in my father's face and then turn around years later and embrace the whole thing. She told me she was a witch too. I still don't get it."

Agnes took a sip of her shake and shrugged. "I've known your mother and her sister their whole lives. It's a small town so you get a feel for people. Rachel was the sweetest thing I'd ever met. That's who you get your red hair from. But she was too sweet, if you know what I mean. She saw nothing but the good in people and sometimes that can hurt you. Lena was always jealous of her sister. She wasn't a bad person then, but she always wanted what Rachel had. And that included you. She wanted a child so badly and when she saw her chance, she took advantage of your father's grief and took what she wanted. So that was the beginning of her downward spiral. The cause of that spiral? I think it involves Charles. I think he's back and I think he knows about you and wants to use you just like he wanted to use your father. Race disagrees, but I have a feeling about this. You've gotta be careful girl. Time to start watching your back."

Sarah rubbed her forehead as a headache started to form. "So the same guy that killed my mom might be after me now? Well, that's just great," she said tiredly and stared out the window at all the normal people walking by with normal problems and normal lives. Normal just wasn't a category she fit in.

"Um, speaking of people who are after me, how are they? How are Lena and Drake and those women?" she wondered for the first time if it was possible she'd actually killed anyone.

Agnes shook her head, reading her thoughts easily. "They're fine and in jail where they deserve to be. That man Drake has electrical burns on his shoulders and neck, but everyone else is fine. They're being charged with kidnapping and attempted murder."

Sarah's eyebrows shot up and she sat up straight, looking at Agnes in horror. "You're kidding me," she whispered.

Agnes shook her head, suddenly very grave. "They're going through all of Drake's journals now and interrogating everyone, but from all the facts they have at this moment, they came real close to killing Zane. They're doing what they can to keep them in jail until they have all the facts. No bail has been set."

Sarah felt cold and exposed all of a sudden and wished she were with Zane. "And my father? Race. What about him? Did he just disappear into the shadows again?"

Agnes looked at her carefully and then sighed. "Race came by the store this morning. He and I had a long talk. He still doesn't feel like he can be your father because of what happened to your mom. But he feels that you need watching over. I think seeing those women come close to shooting you woke something up in him, which is one good thing to come out of this mess. That man needed a cold bucket of reality if you ask me. He says he can't be your father, but I don't buy it. He just doesn't know how. He says he'd like to talk to you when you're ready."

Sarah looked away as the waiter brought the bill. Agnes paid with her credit card and they left the restaurant. Agnes drove her to the hospital in silence, knowing that Sarah was busy processing everything.

"I'll park the car. You go on up. It's the third floor, room 328. Go on," she urged, with a wave of her hands.

Sarah smiled gratefully and ran into the hospital, slowing to a walk as she followed the signs to the elevator. She rode the elevator impatiently, wishing she had just taken the stairs when the doors finally opened onto the third floor. She ran right into Gretchen.

Gretchen stepped back, laughing, her eyes bright and sparkly with happiness. "I was just coming to get you! I told my mom to tell you that I'd be there at 4 to pick you up. It's just three now."

Sarah shrugged. "I think she knew I wanted to see how Zane was doing. She's down parking the car right now."

Gretchen patted her on the shoulder and reached out to grab the elevator door to keep it from closing. "Perfect. She can go with me to the police station. Will you be okay hanging out here with Zane for a couple hours?"

Sarah grinned, nodding her head. "Of course. See you later," she said and hurried towards Zane's room.

She entered the room and looked at Zane who was pushing the button on his remote to move his bed into a sitting position.

She rushed to his side and threw her arms around his neck, hugging him tightly. "How are you feeling?" she asked pulling away and sitting on the side of his bed.

Zane looked tired and his color was still off, but he was grinning happily at her. "I'm feeling fine. The Dr.'s say that I've suffered a lot of damage to my liver and kidneys, but that I should be okay. They're flushing my system right now," he said with a grimace.

Sarah winced and looked at the bags of liquid hooked to his IV. She'd barely noticed them when she'd rushed in. But now all she could see was all of the equipment surrounding him.

"I must not have done a very good job yesterday," she said regretfully wondering why she hadn't been able to purge him completely of the drugs.

Zane shook his head at her. "Sarah, you saved my life. They gave me enough drugs to kill two people. Everyone is stunned that I'm even alive. They're going to test my liver and kidneys in a little while and they say if everything comes back good, they're going to send me home," he said looking out the window wistfully.

Sarah reached out and grabbed his hand in hers. "I could try again."

Zane turned and looked at her hopefully. "I didn't want to ask. Mom told me how worn out you were from saving me yesterday, but I've gotta get out of here Sarah. It's driving me crazy."

Sarah frowned over her shoulder at the open door, leading out to the hallway.

"Not very much privacy here, is there?" she asked wondering how she was going to do what she needed to do.

Zane looked at the door, frowning and it swung shut with a loud click. Sarah tilted her head and smiled at him. "Wow, you are feeling better."

Zane tried to look pitiful. "Just not good enough though. Please, Sarah?" he said, clasping his hands together and trying hard to look pathetic.

Sarah rolled her eyes. "Fine, but this is just a little awkward. You're wearing a backless hospital gown and I need to touch where your kidneys and liver are."

Zane laughed not looking embarrassed at all. "My lucky day. Just come sit down by me and wrap your arms around me like you did yesterday. I don't think it matters where you put your hands."

Sarah blushed feeling embarrassed all of a sudden. As she looked into his silver eyes, the thought that she'd almost lost him yesterday felt overwhelming. "Zane," she whispered and got a lump in her throat.

Zane leaned forward, wrapping his arms around her. "It's over. It's okay now."

Sarah rested her head against his strong shoulder and felt a couple tears drip onto his gown. Her hands went around his back and she sighed as his warmth wrapped around her. She closed her eyes and without even trying, felt her energy melt into Zane. She thought the word *cleanse* and *purify* in her mind and then inched closer, sighing peacefully.

They sat there, wrapped in each other's arms until they heard a polite knock on the door followed by a vigorous rattle. Sarah glanced at her watch and noticed that at least a half an hour had passed by. She pulled away from Zane and got up to sit on a chair by the bed.

Zane called out, "Come in."

The door rattled again and a man's voice called out. "It's locked. I can't open it."

Zane looked hard at the door and watched as it swung open, revealing a doctor in blue scrubs holding a clip board. He stared at the door reproachfully and opened and closed it himself testing the latch.

"I'll have to get maintenance up here. That could be dangerous. So, how are you feeling Zane?" he asked kindly, glancing down at the clip board and back up.

Zane smiled at Sarah. "I've never felt better. As a matter of fact, I do believe I'm ready to go home."

The doctor glanced at Sarah and smiled wider. "I can see why. Why don't we go ahead and have the nurse take your blood for the tests and we'll see if we can't get you out of here. Maybe there's still time to catch a movie if things look good."

Zane grinned and thanked the Doctor. Sarah stepped out of the room while they took the blood. She wandered over to the pop machine and put in some change for a Dr. Pepper.

"Sarah."

Sarah turned around and saw that her father was standing a few feet away. She swallowed nervously and reached down to get her drink.

"Hi. What are you doing here?" she asked, opening the drink and taking a sip.

Race stared at her curiously before answering. "To see Zane of course. I wanted to make sure he was okay."

Sarah nodded and looked at the floor, not knowing what to say to this man who had willfully chosen to not be a part of her life.

"I've always loved you Sarah," Race said, looking down at his feet.

Sarah looked up and stared at her father's bent head. She frowned, feeling angry for some reason. "Well, you have a really strange way of showing it," she bit out, feeling an electrical pulse slip down her arm.

Race looked at her arm and then smiled gently at her. "I know and I'm sorry. Seeing you up close, yesterday and here right now, I can see your mother in you. And I can see me too. And what I can't see, I can feel," he said wonderingly.

Sarah looked away as a pain she faintly remembered hurt her heart.

Race ran his hand through his short dark hair and looked impatient. With himself or her, she didn't know.

"I know I've messed up, but I'd like to make things right between us. I can't change the past, but maybe we could get to know one another."

Sarah took another sip of her drink and looked at her feet. "I guess. Maybe," she said, sounding unsure.

Race smiled and nodded as if she'd jumped up and shouted *Yes!* "That's great. I have a lot I can teach you about your power. You're not like most witches and neither am I. That's a good thing but it can be dangerous too," he said and then frowned, his face falling as a deep sadness came into his eyes.

Sarah watched him as he bunched his fists and shoved them into his jeans pockets.

"I'd be interested to learn what I can."

Race looked up, his face clearing slowly. He smiled and reached out to touch her arm. "That's good then. I'll be in touch," he said and turned to walk into Zane's room.

Sarah sighed and rolled her shoulders. That had been weird. She walked over to the waiting room and picked up a magazine. She flipped through it as the nurses walked out with their cart full of Zane's blood. Twenty minutes later, Race walked out, waved at her and then walked towards the elevators. She stood up to go see Zane but stopped when Gretchen and Agnes walked out of the elevator, holding bags of goodies and books and DVD's in their hands.

"Sarah! What are you doing out here? You're supposed to be in there keeping Zane from going crazy," Gretchen chided

"Race just left. I thought I'd give them some time to chat."

Sarah smiled and glanced at the bag in Gretchen's hands. "Those wouldn't happen to be apple fritters would they?"

Gretchen opened the bag and handed her one. "Zane's favorite. I got three just in case you were hungry.

Agnes laughed and shook her head. "I don't know where you're putting it after that steak you had for lunch."

Sarah grinned munching happily on the donut. "I burned that up about a half an hour ago. They say they'll release Zane if his blood tests come back good."

Gretchen's raised her eyebrows. "Did you . . .?"

Sarah nodded. "Yeah, but it wasn't as draining as yesterday. His blood still had traces of the drug though. I could feel it ooze out of his pores."

Agnes smiled approvingly. "Your father used to be a good healer years ago. I remember Hal Petersen collapsed at the grocery store one day. He had a grand mal seizure or something and your dad ran over and just barely rubbed his hand over Hals' head and he stopped seizing. It was the most amazing thing I'd ever seen. And then he patted Hal on the shoulder and left the store. Most people had no idea what he'd done, but I felt the energy current. I knew he'd stopped the seizure."

Sarah looked at her feet, feeling curious about the father who was more of a stranger to her. Gretchen opened the door for Agnes and Sarah.

"Come on you two. I can feel Zane waiting for us very impatiently," she said with a grin.

An hour later Zane was released from the hospital. Gretchen took him straight home to rest and Sarah accompanied Agnes to the store. As Agnes pulled her keys out of her pocket, Lash stepped out of the shadows.

Sarah jumped in surprise but then frowned when she saw Lash's face. Something was wrong.

Chapter 17 - Rush

"Hey Agnes, can you give me a half hour? This is my friend Lash. I really need to talk to him," Sarah said, motioning to Lash who was standing behind her, and slouching down.

Agnes peered around Sarah and looked piercingly at Lash. Her dark gray eyebrows went straight up to her hair line. She blinked a few times and then looked at Sarah worriedly. "*Sarah . . .*," she said in a strained voice.

Sarah stepped in close to Agnes and touched her arm. "It's okay Agnes. He's a friend. I'll be back as soon as I can."

Agnes bit her lip but nodded. Sarah turned around, grabbed Lash's arm and pulled him down the sidewalk. After they were out of eyesight from the store, Sarah slowed down and glanced at Lash. He looked miserable, more so than she'd ever seen him before.

"I know of a good place we can talk privately. Scared of the woods?" she asked with a faint smile.

Lash looked up at her and shook his head, still not saying anything. Lash looked too tired for a run, so they walked for fifteen minutes in silence until they came to Sarah's tree house.

"Have you ever climbed a tree before?" Sarah asked, jumping up to grab the first limb. She pulled herself quickly up the tree and onto the floor of the tree house. Lash joined her seconds later.

Sarah leaned her back up against the trunk while Lash huddled in the corner. She leaned over and grabbed her sleeping bag that had been left behind and tossed it to him.

"You look kind of cold. Lash, what's going on? We all heard about Jill's murder and that the police were questioning you. Zane told me that Charity gave you an alibi though. Are you cleared?" she asked, wishing Lash would look her in the eyes.

Lash slowly raised his head and his bright blue eyes were swimming in tears. Sarah winced and scooted over to put her arm around his shoulders.

"Lash, I'm so sorry," she said.

Lash quickly wiped his eyes and breathed slowly in and out a few times as he tried to gain control of himself.

"I didn't kill her Sarah. You believe me right?" he asked softly.

Sarah patted his shoulder and pulled her arm back. "Of course I believe you. Nobody else believes you did it either. Charity told everyone she was with you."

Lash nodded. "Yeah, but I just wanted to know if you did. I don't care what anyone else thinks. But I couldn't handle it if you thought I had."

Sarah looked at her feet and clasped her hands over her knees. "So do they know what happened? Do they have any idea who killed her?" she prodded gently.

Lash shook his head and looked out over the woods. "Nah. They're still trying to pin it on me, but the DNA doesn't match and I have an alibi. But I know who did it," he said, his voice wavering slightly.

Sarah turned quickly and grabbed his hand excitedly. "That's great Lash! Who is it? We can help point the police in the right direction before it happens again."

Lash ran his free hand through his hair and sighed before turning to face Sarah. "I think it was my dad. He's back Sarah. He's been in the city because he can get blood there anytime he wants and because I won't give it to him anymore. But I can tell he's been in the house. Little things like books that have been moved or papers. And his cologne. I can smell it sometimes," he said in a hoarse voice filled with dread.

Sarah blinked a few times, feeling her heart squeeze painfully for Lash. "You're sure it wasn't the maid?" she asked, hoping Lash was just imagining things.

Lash shook his head, his face turning hard. "Positive. I've told her she can clean the bathroom and change the sheets in my room, but she's not allowed to touch any of my personal stuff. It was like someone did a search through all of my things. And I would recognize that scent anywhere Sarah. I know it's him. He's here, he's lying low and he's up to something. I think he killed Jill because he thinks I loved her or something. His little way of getting revenge on me for not giving him what he wants."

Sarah let out a long breath and massaged her forehead. "Well, first things first. You shouldn't stay at your house anymore. You're not safe there. I had to move recently because of the same thing."

Lash rolled his eyes. "In case you haven't noticed Sarah, my life isn't a Disney movie. I don't have the good natured best friend, whose mom likes to feed me and loves me like a second son."

Sarah winced and then laughed softly. "Too true. But I think I know someone who will take you in," she said, hoping she was right.

Lash shook his head. "I'm not moving in with Zane. I'd probably end up killing him."

Sarah punched him the arm, smiling. "No, not Zane. My father. Race Livingston."

Lash pulled away and turned to look at her closely. "*No way.* Race Livingston is your father? He's that really strange guy that lives on the edge of town, right?"

Sarah shrugged and nodded. "Yeah, he's a little different, but let's face it, so are you Lash."

Lash nodded, looking uneasy and nervous. "It wouldn't hurt to ask because you're right. I can't sleep anymore. I just don't feel safe at home. I don't know what I'll do if my father tries to use me again," he said, flexing his hands into fists and sounding agitated.

Sarah sighed in misery for her friend. "We'll go straight there. I'll introduce you to him. It'll be okay."

Lash swallowed slowly and looked up at her. "And if he says no?"

Sarah grinned. "Then you and Zane will have that Disney Movie moment. Who knows, maybe he has bunk beds?" she said teasingly.

Lash groaned good-naturedly but then leaned his head back against the old wood of the tree house. "Jill's dead now because of my father. He's such a freaking monster. And to think I was on my way to becoming just like him," he said sounding horrified at himself.

Sarah got up on her knees in front of Lash and reached over to shake his shoulders. "Lash, knock it off. You made some serious mistakes, but you're not like your dad. It's your choice who you become. You will *not* be like him."

Lash lowered his head. "I took some blood from Charity. She didn't even know it. It wasn't much, just a little."

Sarah let go of Lash's shoulders and sat back on her heels and stared at Lash pityingly.

"Well, maybe I'm wrong then. Maybe you will be a monster just like your dad."

Lash whipped his head up and glared at her, breathing fast and turning red. "Never! I'll never be like that. I'll never take blood again. Every time I'm tempted, I just think of Jill. It's been two days Sarah. I've been clean for 2 days. I've read the 12 steps over and over. I'm done with step one and I'm on step #2. I refuse to be a monster like him Sarah. I'd rather die," he swore.

Sarah breathed a sigh of relief and smiled. "Then that's settled. Why don't we go find my dad so we can introduce you?"

Lash looked at her, his eyes torn with emotion. His breathing calmed down and his shoulders relaxed finally. "You did that on purpose, didn't you?"

Sarah tilted her head and raised her eyebrows. "Whatever it takes Lash," she said and moved towards the opening of the tree house.

"Wait Sarah. What about you? There was some gossip on Facebook today that Zane was kidnapped and that some guy tried to kill you. I didn't believe it of course, but that's why I came by the bookstore. I wanted to make sure you were okay."

Sarah grimaced and sat back down. She didn't know what to tell Lash. She didn't know of anyone who'd believe what really happened. Even Lash with his family's blood lust tradition might have his mind blown by the thought of what she could do and what other people would do to her because of it. She'd better edit.

"My aunt got mixed up with a bad group of people. They wanted me to be involved with what they were doing and Zane got in the way. The police came and they're in jail now. It's okay."

Lash raised his eyebrow at her. "It's okay for me to tell you all my deepest darkest secrets but you can't tell me what those jerks wanted you involved in?"

Sarah winced and clasped her hands nervously.

"That bad huh? It's okay Sarah. It took me forever to get the courage to tell someone. Just tell me when you can okay?" he said sympathetically.

Sarah looked up in relief and gratitude. "Okay, deal."

Sarah and Lash made their way down the tree and started walking out of the woods. Lash tried to hold her hand, but she laughed at him and pushed him away.

"Dude, personal space," she warned.

Lash grinned at her. "You can't blame me for trying. I have to warn you I'm very stubborn and I don't give up easily."

Sarah laughed and shook her head as they came to the edge of the woods. A dark form slipped out of the shadows from behind a tree and walked towards them. Sarah didn't think anything of it. There was always a hiker or two coming and going.

She felt Lash stiffen beside her as the shadow came closer. She reached out and grabbed Lash's hand in hers. She knew without Lash saying anything that this was his father. It was the same man that had come into the bookstore who Gretchen and Zane had had such a strong negative reaction to. She felt a cold shiver rip down her spine and her power tingled in her hands. Lash squeezed her hand quickly but then dropped it as he moved to stand in front of her.

"What are you doing here? Were you following me?" Lash demanded, his voice strong and confident.

Sarah reached out a hand to hold onto Lash's arm. Not to keep him back, but to send as much calm and strength to him as she could.

"I know where you are every second of the day. You really get around, don't you Lash? First that girl you wasted. Then that cute blond you were with the other night. And now a pretty red head? Lash, you're going to have to pace yourself," the man said in a cold, amused voice.

Sarah made an insulted sound and moved to get around Lash, but he reached back and with a surprisingly strong grip, kept her behind him.

"I know you killed Jill. Everyone knows she lost a lot of blood. That could only be you," Lash said, anger seething in his voice.

Mason Crossly leaned his head back and laughed, making Sarah feel like throwing up. It was the most evil laugh she'd ever heard. This guy was worse than Drake. Way worse.

"I might have gotten a little carried away. But I figured if she was your snack, you wouldn't mind sharing. You were done with her anyways. There's no use denying it. By the time I found her, she was so used up, there was practically nothing left to her. I'd say we share equally in Jill's demise. Now, why don't you introduce me to this delectable young lady hiding behind you. Don't be rude now Lash. Be polite," he said with a gleam in his eye that had Lash backing up.

Sarah grasped Lash's arms tightly, feeling rivers of unease wash through her body. She leaned up and whispered in Lash's ear. "It's okay. Let me handle this."

Lash looked over his shoulder at her, looking more worried and upset than she'd ever seen him before.

Sarah walked out from behind Lash and stood next to him. Lash immediately put a protective arm around her shoulder. She had to smile a little remembering all the times she had been the one to put a protective arm around him.

"I'm Sarah Hudson. I've heard quite a bit about you. You're a pathetic, murdering monster and you're going to jail. You have my word on that," she said, glaring at him.

Mason grinned at her and stepped closer. Lash snarled at him and held a hand up. "Stay away from her. If you even think about touching her, I'll kill you."

Sarah gulped and turned to stare at Lash. She believed him.

Mason looked a little surprised too. "Well, my boy really is growing up. But like any wild predator, you're going to have to prove yourself if you want to stand in my way."

Sarah ground her teeth, loathing everything about Mason. "You're despicable for what you've done to your son, year after year, using him over and over. You disgust me. I know all about you," she threw at him, feeling more and more energy spark in her blood.

Mason raised an eyebrow and looked at Lash questioningly. "You mentioned Blutrausch to this young lady?"

Lash nodded. "She knows everything you did to me."

Mason grinned and looked pleased. "Good, then what I'm going to do won't come as a shock to her. I assume you've done a good job of breaking her to the bridle."

154

Lash shivered in rage, clenching his fists and looking as if he was going to fly at his father any second. Sarah looked back and forth between the two and realized that that's exactly what Mason wanted Lash to do. She glared at Mason in disgust. She had to take matters into her own hands before Lash got hurt. She focused all her energy into equal parts rage and the desire to protect Lash. She raised her arm and pointed at Mason, sending her energy spinning out of her and towards him.

Mason blinked at her hand curiously but was then blown backwards three feet, landing on his back. He arched his back and let out a roar of rage and pain.

Lash turned and stared at her in surprise. "Did you just . . . *did you do that?*" he asked in awe.

Sarah stared at Mason with a worried frown. He should be quivering on the ground wetting himself but instead he was slowly getting to his feet and brushing the leaves off his pants. He looked furious, he looked unkempt and the most frightening thing of all, he looked totally fine.

"Lash, let's get out of here," she whispered, hoping he could run as fast as she could.

Lash let Sarah pull him backwards towards the short path leading to the street.

"I haven't had a witch in years," Mason said with a voice raspy from excitement. He walked slowly towards them, his eyes glued to Sarah in a hungry way. "There's nothing more delicious or more powerful than a witch's blood. If I had you, I wouldn't need anyone else," he said reverently, reaching out a hand to touch her.

Sarah pulled Lash with her as they kept walking backwards, away from Mason. Lash stared back and forth between Mason and Sarah.

"Sarah isn't a witch. I don't know what just happened here, but she's no witch. Stop looking at her like that," he ordered, practically shouting the last.

Mason paused to look at his son. *"You idiot.* Don't you know what's in front of you? When you tasted her, didn't you feel the power running over your tongue? We'll share." He said and lunged for Sarah, grabbing her shoulders and bringing her towards him.

Lash roared and threw himself on his father, taking him to the ground. Sarah stumbled to the side, slipping on the rocks and leaves and landing heavily on her hip. She groaned and stood up as quickly as she could. Her energy and adrenaline were flowing more powerfully than they ever had before. She could throw more energy at him, but she didn't want to hit Lash. Lash's fists were flying so fast, she could barely see them. But Mason was just as fast and he was landing more hits. Lash was fighting with the desire to protect her, but Mason was fighting to get to her blood. Her heart stuttered in fear as she realized that Mason was starting to gain the upper hand.

Sarah felt ill as she watched the brutal fight. She had left her cell phone back in her room at the store. She didn't know what to do. She circled around the fighters looking for any opening. Mason roared and grabbed Lash and threw him across the clearing into a tree. Lash's head made a sickening thud sound before he fell limply to the ground.

Sarah ran to Lash and quickly sent some of her power into Lash, feeling the injuries to his head and his body. She didn't have time though as Mason wiped a line of blood making its way down his chin onto his hand. He licked it slowly, savoring the taste of his own blood as he walked closer to her. Sarah stood up and screeched as she sent her energy flying at Mason. She thought the word *lacerate* in her mind clearly and then watched as Mason's eyes flew wide in horror. Lines appeared on every visible part of Mason's face, throat and arms. Sarah watched, sickened as the lines turned bright red. Mason held up his hands in horror, staring at them and then at her.

"You're going to wish you hadn't done that." He said in a normal voice and then threw himself at her.

Sarah flung herself to the side, but Mason was too quick and caught her arm. He pulled her to him, ignoring his torn flesh and the blood dripping from his face and arms.

Sarah fought as hard as she could, sending out frantic energy pulses that would have killed someone else, but that weren't even slowing Mason down. She kicked and screamed, falling to the ground. She stared up at him in horror, noticing the blood on his face and arms was already slowing and the wounds closing up. Mason stood over her, gleefully.

"So much spirit and fire. So much untapped power. I'll never let you go. You're going to be mine for a very long time," he said with relish.

Sarah got ready to jump to her feet and run for it when Mason's body flew into the air a few feet. She stared up at him, her mouth hanging open as Mason was upright, stiff, seemingly floating in the air, his head thrown back and his eyes closed.

Sarah scrambled to her feet and looked down at her hands. She hadn't done it. She glanced at Lash, still out cold and then turned around to see Zane walking towards her, staring at Mason with so much hatred in his face she wouldn't have recognized him. His eyes looked like cold shards of metal. Her breath was now coming in gasps as she turned back to stare up at Mason's body again. His head was now hanging limply to the side and his body looked as if it were being held up by wires as if he was some freakish Haunted house dummy.

Sarah tried to say something, but nothing came out. Zane kept his gaze on Mason as he walked slowly towards the body hanging in the air. His face tightened as he raised his hand in Mason's direction and then made his hand in a claw. Sarah watched in horror as Mason's body stiffened horrifically and then crumbled, falling at long last to the ground in a heap.

Sarah walked timidly towards Zane, reaching out her hand to him. He finally tore his gaze away from Mason and reached for her pulling her into his arms.

Sarah sobbed into Zane's chest, her body shaking uncontrollably. "He was going to take my blood," she whispered into his chest.

Zane nodded, smoothing her hair back from her face and kissing her forehead. "I know. I could feel everything that was happening to you. I could feel what he was saying to you. I could even feel what you were seeing, like your thoughts were my thoughts."

Sarah looked up at him in surprise. "But, how?"

Zane shook his head. "I don't know. All I know was that you were in serious trouble and the closer I got to you the clearer everything was."

Sarah shivered and looked at Mason. "Is he dead? Did you kill him?"

Zane walked over and kicked him with his foot so he landed on his back. He closed his eyes for a few seconds and then shook his head. "Unfortunately, no. I can feel his blood still moving."

Sarah walked over and touched Zane's arm. "How did you do that? I mean, your mom told me that you were powerful, but I thought that was just with metal objects."

Zane grimaced and looked at Sarah. "Blood has a lot of Iron in it. I could feel you walking towards me that first day because somehow I could feel your blood calling out to me. I'm in tune with all forms of metal. I can manipulate it. The iron in someone's blood is no different. I can stop it. And if I'm really upset, I can look at a man, pick him up, and cause an aneurism or a heart attack."

Sarah's mouth dropped open. "Is that what you did?"

Zane shook his head. "No, I could feel what he was saying to you Sarah. I want this guy to pay for killing Jill. He's just passed out from lack of oxygen to the brain. I give him fifteen minutes. In the meantime," he said and took out his cellphone. He dialed 911, glancing over at Lash finally.

Sarah wondered how she could have forgotten about him. She ran to Lash's side, pulling him onto his back and resting his head on her lap. She placed her hands on both sides of Lash's head, feeling the blood swelling against the tissues of his brain. He had a pretty serious head injury. She closed her eyes and thought the word *heal* as she felt her energy flow through Lash. She felt the swelling subside slowly.

Zane touched her shoulder gently. "They'll be here any second. Let's get our stories straight. This is the second time in two days that the police are coming to the woods to rescue us. We better start thinking fast."

Sarah felt wobbly, but got to her feet, feeling better about Lash at least. "I don't have a taser this time to blame it on. We could just say we were innocent bystanders between the fight between Lash and his dad. We can say we were here the whole time and heard Mason admit to killing Jill and how he threatened me too. Should we bring up the blood drinking?" she asked, biting her lip nervously.

Zane ran his hands down his jeans, frowning as he heard the sirens come closer. "Crap, I don't know. I think we have to. But I don't want kids at school to know Lash had a problem with it too. He deserves a break."

Sarah felt her heart warm at the compassion she heard in Zane's voice. She walked over, stood on tip toe and kissed his cheek. "You're amazing. And you're sweet. But if Lash tells them what his dad did to him and I tell them what he threatened to do to me and they have all the forensic proof of Jill's body, I think this guy might actually go to jail, which in the end, would mean that Lash could be free from his dad and wouldn't have to look over his shoulder."

Zane nodded his head but turned when he heard Mason groan and attempt to turn on his side. "I can't believe how strong he is. For him to withstand what you were throwing at him and for him to be able to recover this fast is outrageous. He must have had a lot of adrenaline or he was on a blood high."

Sarah felt like gagging. "Yeah, Jill's blood."

Zane's face darkened and he walked over and kicked Mason in the ribs. Mason groaned and fell back on his side. Two police cars pulled up to the sidewalk. Four police officers jumped out of the cars and rushed to their sides. Two of the officers had been there when Zane had been rescued. They looked confused and surprised, but Zane took charge of the situation, gesturing to Lash and Mason. One police officer radioed for an ambulance.

Mason took that opportunity to roll to his side and jump to his feet. He stumbled at first but then started running back towards the woods. Zane took off after him and used his power over Mason's blood to bring him down into submission again.

Zane stood up, wiping his hands on the back of his jeans as the police officers caught up, their weapons drawn and pointed at Mason.

"I think I knocked him out when I tackled him," he said, sounding apologetic.

Officer Davis, the one with a buzz cut and who looked like a big bear smiled at that. "No apology needed kid."

They cuffed Mason and hauled him to the back of the police car. The ambulance arrived and Sarah watched worriedly as they strapped Lash to the stretcher and placed him in the ambulance. Gretchen and Agnes, followed by Race arrived then, standing back and looking grim as Sarah and Zane gave the officers their statements. When Zane told them Mason had bragged about killing Jill, the black officer made a quick call back to the precinct.

Sarah grabbed the police officer's arm as he put his radio back in the clip. "Those cuffs won't hold him officer. He's incredibly strong."

The officer laughed and shook his head. "He was just taken down by your boyfriend here pretty easily. He's not that tough. Don't you worry about it."

Sarah and Zane ended up being escorted to the police station where they were separated to give their statements again. A few hours later, Gretchen insisted on taking them home. Sarah was grateful to escape and slumped against the leather seat in the back as Zane held her hand.

"Do you know what Officer Davis said to me? I can't get it out of my head," she murmured.

Zane rubbed his thumb comfortingly along the back of her hand. "What?"

Sarah stared unseeingly out the window, surprised at how dark the night was. "He said, it's so funny that all of this crazy stuff is happening right now and you've been involved in both situations. He said that it couldn't be a coincidence."

Zane frowned and nodded. "Well, he might have a point, but regardless of your bad luck, they told my mom that Lash is awake and doing great at the hospital. He gave his statement and corroborated what we told them. Mason's going down. They'll do the DNA testing right away. He's going to prison for killing Jill. There's no way he's getting away with it now."

Sarah nodded but felt uneasy. She couldn't forget how easily he'd recovered from her energy attacks. "Do you really think a prison will hold him?"

Zane sighed heavily and sat back against the seat. "They laughed me off when I told him how strong he was. But after explaining about the blood lust, they checked the back of Lash's neck. They know we're telling the truth about that. Whether or not they take the right precautions is up to them now. If he does get out? I'll be right here," he swore softly.

Sarah looked at him quickly and scooted over to his side, leaning in to his arm. "I don't want you anywhere near him Zane. You should have seen him when he realized what I was. He was inflamed at the idea of getting my blood. He probably thinks he collapsed because of something I did. He might not know you're a witch. If he does, and he gets out, I'm worried he'll come for you."

Zane looked down at her with a wince covered by a small smile. "Your faith in my abilities to protect you and myself is kind of humbling Sarah. And not in a good way."

Sarah laughed. "That's not what I meant. We both know you're not invincible. Drugs are not your friend."

Zane groaned and slouched down further, putting his arm over Sarah's shoulder. "I'll agree with you on that. But I think I proved today that I'm a good back up."

161

Sarah kissed his cheek and snuggled closer. "That you did. I just don't want you to become a target."

Zane's eyes went cold and mean. "You mean, like you?"

Sarah sighed tiredly. "Yeah. Like me."

Chapter 18 - The Friend Zone

The next three days were taken up with trips to the police station, the hospital and going back to school. She worked when she could but knew in her heart that she wasn't doing a good job of earning her keep. When she brought the subject up to Gretchen, she looked at her like she was insane.

"Earning your keep? Saving my son's life earned your keep for the next three hundred years. Your using an empty room that no one else needed or wanted, is no big deal. Besides, the store is doing so well with the added boutique and art and pastries that we've talked about giving you a little raise."

Sarah laughed and held her hands up. "Not until I earn it. I forbid you."

Gretchen laughed and shooed her out the door. She hitched her backpack over her shoulders and wished Zane could have given her a ride to school that morning but he'd gone in early to make up a test he had missed while he was in the hospital.

She felt the cool fall air slide around her face and through her wavy hair and let herself smile. The colors of the changing leaves lightened her heart and she wondered, *no hoped*, that the rest of the year would be good. Her aunt and her friends were behind bars for now. Lash was safe from his dad and Jill would have justice. She also happened to have a gorgeous boyfriend. It wasn't official, but everyone at school assumed they were together. Heck, Zane assumed they were. And on top of that, she had a job and people in her life who cared about her. She was starting to understand herself and her power better. She still didn't understand her father and their relationship but was willing to give it some time. All in all? Not so bad.

She was coming into her own. She was finding out who she really was and she was strangely happy. She grinned at her reflection as she walked past a shop window and liked what she saw. An attractive, happy girl with a good future ahead of her. She'd never seen that before.

She looked both ways and then crossed the street, jumping up onto the sidewalk as a car came around the corner. She readjusted her back pack and glanced at the car as it started to slow down. It was a sleek, gray Mercedes with tinted windows. She couldn't see through the windows, but she could feel something cold coming from inside.

She looked away quickly and got as far away from the street as she could. The car pulled to the side of the street and she heard a car door open behind her. She sighed and shook her head. She was not in the mood to deal with anymore crap. Without looking behind her, she leapt into a run and disappeared into the crowd of other teenagers heading in the same direction. When she was surrounded by people she took a second and turned her head to look back. On the street corner she had just left, stood a tall man with bright blond hair, wearing a trench coat and sunglasses. He was looking right at her. She could feel it. She glared at the man, tempted to send a little electricity his way just for ruining her happy moment but decided against it. It was probably nothing.

She joined Zane in 1st period and thought about mentioning it to him, but decided not to when she saw how happy and carefree he looked. She didn't want to ruin his day with her gloomy feelings of paranoia. Besides, it was just some guy standing on a street corner. People did that all the time. Did they pull their cars over, get out and attempt to follow her? No. But the standing part was completely normal and so she was going to grasp on to that.

The rest of the day was normal and as she sat next to Zane at lunch time, cocooned in his warmth she let the rest of her worries go. She was going to push all her misgivings away. She didn't want them. She wanted happiness. Lash walked up and put his tray down on their table, pulling a chair over to join them.

Lash even looked happy. His eyes were bright and clear and his shoulders were relaxed. For the first time in his life, he looked like he should. Like a good looking kid, enjoying high school. Sarah grinned at him, letting go of Zane's hand.

"How's your head Lash?" she asked, knowing already that it was perfectly good.

"I'm good as new. No headaches even. I talked to the District Attorney last night and he's taking this case very seriously. There was a case of blood lust up in Canada last year. It didn't make the papers down here, but it was big news. The guy went after little kids walking home from kindergarten. They put him away for three consecutive life sentences. He thinks my dad might get something similar if I testify."

Zane frowned and sat forward. "You up to that?"

Lash nodded firmly. "I'm doing it for myself, but mostly for Jill. I'll do whatever it takes to make sure he pays for taking her life."

Sarah winced, feeling the weight of what was ahead of him. "What about bail? Gretchen told me his lawyer was trying to get him free until the trial begins," she said sharing a worried glance with Zane.

Lash shook his head and opened up his coke. "Nah, after he broke that guard's arm when he attempted to escape that first night, they know he's a flight risk. I think we're safe," he said with such a feeling of relief that Sarah reached over and grabbed his hand, squeezing it warmly.

"People just don't realize how wonderful that feeling is. We do." She said softly.

Lash looked at her, his blues eyes turning soft as he put his other hand over the top of hers. "You always made me feel safe."

Zane cleared his throat and grabbed Sarah's other hand. Sarah pulled her hand away from Lash, blushing as she saw Zane's raised eyebrow.

"So what's next for you Lash? Where do you go from here?" Zane asked, trying to move the conversation to safer ground.

Lash pulled his eyes away from Sarah and looked at Zane considering. "I might take over my father's business. He owns a water bottling company. I've been in contact with his business associates. After graduation I'll be heading to the city, unless something keeps me here," he said glancing back at Sarah.

Sarah decided it would be much safer if she just ate her sandwich. They both got the hint and talked about colleges and careers for a while.

"Hi Lash."

Everyone looked up to see Charity standing next to their table with one of her friends standing at a safe distance behind her. Sarah smiled at her since she had given Lash his alibi. Lash smiled at her, but looked kind of strained too.

"Hey Charity, how's it going?" he asked.

"Um, I was wondering if you were free after school? I've got a project for English due and I could really use some help on it. My mom and dad are in town and they wanted me to invite you to dinner. They'd really like to meet you," she said looking hopeful and kind of vulnerable too.

Lash looked down at the floor for a few minutes and then cleared his throat. "That's really sweet, but I'm going to have to pass. I have to meet with the lawyers after school and then I have to meet with the real estate agent back at the house to get it ready to sell. Good luck with your project though."

Charity's face fell and she nodded. "Okay, I understand. Well, um, see ya around," she said and turned to walk off with her friend.

Sarah felt kind of bad for her. "Is that true, about the lawyers and the house?" Sarah asked, still watching Charity.

166

Lash crumpled up his garbage and shook his head. "I still don't trust myself right now. I don't want her in harm's way. I think in a few months' time I'll be able to go out and socialize like normal guys do. But until then, it's just not worth it."

Sarah smiled sadly at her friend. But Zane was the one who stood up and reached his hand across the table. "You're all right Lash. Friends?"

Lash stood up and glanced at Sarah hesitantly first but then relaxed and shook Zane's hands. No bone crushing this time. The two young men grinned at each other as Zane sat back down. Sarah felt her heart warm as she smiled at Lash.

"Hey Sarah, do you mind if I talk to you in private?" he asked, grabbing his tray and not looking at Zane.

Zane raised his eyebrow at her but shrugged.

Sarah stood up. "Of course. You can walk me to my locker. I'll see ya later Zane."

They dumped their trash and walked out into the busy corridor. "Let's go in here to talk. It's too noisy out here." Lash said and opened the chemistry lab door.

Sarah walked in the room and sat down at one of the front desks. Lash stood in front of her with his arms crossed over his chest. He looked down at her solemnly before speaking.

"I've been meaning to talk to you about this, but I just wasn't sure how to bring it up. So I'm just going to say it. Sarah, was my dad right? Are you a witch?"

Sarah looked up at Lash, and saw the concern in his bright blue eyes and sighed. "Yes and no. Some people might call me a witch, but I don't label myself that way. I have a few different forms of psychokinesis. I can do things that other people can't."

Lash's eyes widened, but he nodded and stepped back to lean against the teacher's desk. "When my dad called you a witch and went crazy on you, I didn't believe it. But then you threw him back without even touching him. And later I started thinking of all the times you stuck up for me and weird things would happen. Was that you using your power?"

Sarah ran a hand through her hair and looked away. "Yeah. Not at first though. I just stuck up for you the old fashioned way when we were young, but when I was about fourteen, I realized I could do more. Are you okay with that?" she asked, looking back at him.

Lash looked at his feet for a moment and then back up at her. "Well, it makes sense now. I just always thought that you were my lucky charm. I never realized that you were doing all of that stuff on purpose. So when Rod threw up my hamburger? You?"

Sarah laughed sheepishly and crossed her legs. "Guilty. But I can't say that I regret it."

Lash grinned and then came closer to her, grabbing a chair and sitting by her side. "I won't tell anyone Sarah. I wouldn't want anyone to look at you differently or judge you or anything," he said touching her silver bracelet with his finger.

Sarah smiled. "Thanks but people already look at me differently. They might not know what I can do, but they can sense it. I'm not exactly Miss Popularity around here."

Lash grinned, his long black hair falling over his eye. "I wouldn't have it any other way. Does, um, does Zane know?" he asked, sitting back and looking curious.

Sarah bit her lip. She was fine with Lash knowing about her, but Zane hadn't given her permission to share his secret. She'd just have to tread carefully.

"Yeah, he knows. The first day of school when we were in class, he confronted me about being a witch. I had to set him straight on that, but yeah, he knows I can do certain things."

Lash frowned and looked disappointed. "Oh well, I was just wondering. Some people can't handle the strange and different."

Sarah laughed and stood up. "Strange and different. That's us Lash. Come on, the bell is going to ring any second."

Lash walked with her to the door, but paused and put his hand on the door as she tried to open it.

"The other thing I wanted to talk to you about . . . was me."

Sarah felt her stomach drop as she looked up into Lash's blue eyes and saw the look there. She moved back a little and cleared her throat nervously.

"Lash, you're gorgeous, you're amazing and you're my friend. But I'm kind of seeing Zane right now. You know that."

Lash reached out and touched her collar bone with his finger, tracing the bone and pale skin with his finger.

"But you never gave me a fair chance. I'm clean now. I'm free. I want to be with you Sarah. I'll always want to be with you."

Sarah gulped and wished he'd stop touching her. She noticed her energy field was completely quiet. Lash was telling the truth. He was clean and free. Yikes, this was all on her now. She wondered faintly if Zane was connected to what she was thinking and feeling right now. Lash might be in trouble if he was.

"Lash, that's the most flattering thing anyone's ever said to me. If I'd never met Zane, of course I'd want to date you, but I did meet Zane. I really like him. I like you too Lash. A lot. But I'm not the type of girl who can like two boys at the same time *in that way*."

Lash smiled sadly and let his head lean against the door as he studied her. "There's no one else like you. You're the only girl I've ever loved. Please don't break my heart."

Sarah's eyes went round and her mouth fell open.

Lash reached out and grasped her waist lightly, pulling her gently closer as he leaned down and tilted his head.

"*Lash*," she whispered pushing against his chest.

Sarah turned her head to the side, so he ended up kissing the side of her mouth, but before she could catch her breath, he had repositioned himself and began kissing her fully.

Sarah squeaked and shoved him harder. He finally pulled back, staring broodingly down at her. Lash's eyes looked electrical blue and the desire on his face told her everything. She reached out and touched his cheek softly.

"I don't know what the future holds Lash. Maybe someday we'll be together. But right now, we're not. As much as I like you, I can't let you do that again. Please just be my friend Lash," she pleaded.

Lash growled low in his throat and looked away, closing his eyes in pain. "You're asking the impossible of me. There's only one thing I feel for you Sarah and it's not friendship. It never will be."

Sarah crossed her arms over her chest and breathed out slowly. "It's friendship or nothing Lash. Please don't choose nothing."

Lash turned and banged his head against the door. Hard. "I'll think about it." He muttered and pushed the door open hard enough to break the hinges and walked quickly out and down the hall.

Sarah walked back to the chair and sat down, resting her head on her arms. She'd never wanted to be one of those girls who had all the boys after her. In all of her fairytales she weaved for herself, there was only one prince. No one else had mattered and she definitely hadn't been torn between two men. She had to admit that Lash did pull at her. He was so different than Zane. Zane was all light and warmth and power. But Lash had a pull on her heart that went back over a decade. And the man he was becoming was very attractive. She'd be lying if she didn't admit it.

Sarah moaned and sat up, sliding out of the chair as the bell rang. She much preferred things to be black and white. All of this gray stuff was giving her a head ache. She opened the door slowly and wasn't surprised to see Zane standing there. He didn't look happy.

"Have a nice chat?" he asked politely.

Sarah winced and wanted to pull her hair out. They turned and headed towards her locker. "What exactly did you feel or hear?" she asked instead of answering the question.

Zane touched her locker and it opened for her. She didn't even bat an eyelash as she grabbed a couple text books.

"I was having a perfectly wonderful conversation with Bryan about going to a party next week and then all of a sudden, my mind was filled with certain images of you getting kissed. As you're aware, when you're feeling a certain strong emotion, I can feel it too."

Sarah shut the door and twirled the lock. She looked down at her shoes and sighed. "What emotion were you picking up on?" she asked miserably.

Zane leaned against her locker and stared at the kids walking through the hallways.

"I believe there was surprise at first. I think on two counts. One that he was a good kisser and two that your energy wasn't pushing him away. The other emotion that I picked up on was that you loved him," Zane said quietly and with a voice laced with pain.

Sarah whipped her head up and grabbed Zane's arm. "You already knew I loved Lash. I've always been clear that I've cared for him."

Zane looked sadly down at her. "Yeah, but that caring can easily turn into something more passionate. And you know it."

Sarah swallowed a lump in her throat and looked away. "I told him that I was with you and that I just wanted to be friends with him."

Zane nodded. "I picked up on that too. I also heard that door slam from across the school. Lash is never going to give up until you and he are together."

Sarah felt so miserable she wished she could disappear. "Zane I don't know what you want me to say. I didn't want him to kiss me. I tried to push him away. I told him that we could only be friends. You know I care about you."

Zane sighed and shoved his hands in his pockets. "I really don't like the idea of having a girlfriend whose heart is split in two."

Sarah felt even worse because she knew deep down, she couldn't deny it. "Maybe we should break up. Not that I'm even officially your girlfriend or anything, but maybe for a while, we should cool things off and step back until we can figure it all out."

Zane frowned, his eyes turning into bright shards of glass. "Is that what you want Sarah? You want to put me back in the friend zone and keep both of us chasing after you?"

Sarah's eyes narrowed at Zane and she stepped back from him. "That's pretty insulting. You're the one who just said he didn't want a girlfriend who had feelings for another guy. You know what? Why don't you just go chase someone else," she said and turned around, stomping down the hallway.

Oooohhh. The nerve of him saying that to her, she fumed. She stopped all of a sudden as if someone had just put their arm around her waist. She looked down and saw nothing. She urged herself forward but didn't go anywhere. Her body was moving backwards, sliding across the scratched, gray linoleum back towards Zane. She fought it hard, baring her teeth and using all of her muscles to force herself to go where she wanted to. She moved an inch. She knew people were starting to look at her funny but she didn't care. She was truly pissed now. She looked back over her shoulder at Zane who was staring at her with no expression on his face.

"I give you three seconds to let me go or you're going to get hurt," she warned very willing to zap him. He had crossed the line.

Zane's eyes narrowed at the threat and she flew backwards into his arms. He held her gently as he swooped in to kiss her. She pushed him back with her hands as she heard cat calls and whooping sounds surrounding them. She pulled back but he followed her, kissing her more and more deeply. Her power betrayed her and flew out of her to surround Zane as his enveloped her at the same time. She gave up and gave in to the kiss, letting all the fury and hurt drain out of her.

Zane finally pulled back and let her down to stand on her own feet. She felt weak and wobbly and had to hold on to his waist for a few minutes. She looked up at him, still glaring.

"I've just decided that you're worth it. I'll chase you if that's what you want. If Lash is fighting for you, then he has a battle on his hands. One he's going to lose. You're mine and you were mine the first day you walked into class. You know it and I know it. Don't let him pull you away from me Sarah. We belong together," he said, pulling her close and talking softly into her ear so no one could over hear.

Sarah collapsed against Zane's chest, resting her head against his shoulder. Her arms wrapped around his waist as she gave in to his warmth.

She didn't say anything but she stood up on her tip toes and kissed him on the lips softly. "I hope you win."

Zane narrowed his eyes at her but then shook his head and grinned. "You know, my life was kind of boring before I met you."

Sarah snorted and smiled. "Come on, we're going to be late."

Zane walked her to her class and then ran down the hall to his as the second bell rang. She watched him disappear and smiled slightly. Who wanted boring?

Chapter 19 - Vacation

After school, she walked towards the parking lot, holding Zane's hand but stopped in surprise when she saw her father leaning against Zane's jeep. She dropped Zane's hand and frowned.

"Uh, *hi*. What are you doing here?"

Race stood up and walked towards them, looking more grim and serious than usual. "I wanted to make sure you two were okay. Mason Crossly just made bail. His lawyer got him out on $100,000.00."

Sarah gasped and looked at Zane who looked just as horrified. "We've gotta find Lash right now," he said, turning his head to scan the parking lot.

Race held up his hand. "No worries. Gretchen just picked him up out front and she has him at the store."

Zane frowned and rubbed his chin. "That can't be safe. I love my mom, but I don't know if she stands a chance against Mason. He's too powerful. If Sarah can't stop him, what can she do?" he asked worriedly.

Race smiled, making Zane pause. "Maybe not on her own, but put us all together and he's got a fight on his hands. He's not stupid. Lash will be fine. Come on; let's go to the store so we can discuss this new development. Sarah? Why don't you ride with me?" he asked, motioning towards a large black SUV parked behind Zane's jeep.

Sarah glanced at Zane, wanting to be with him. She always felt safe and protected when she was with him. And right now, she really, really wanted to feel safe. But she nodded and walked towards her father's car. Zane walked with her and kissed her on the forehead before she hopped up.

"Don't worry. I'll always protect you," he promised and then walked away from her.

Sarah felt comforted and was able to shut the door and put on her seat belt. Race got in and started the car, glancing at her curiously.

"You and Zane look like you're kind of serious. How long have you been dating?" he asked as he pulled out of the parking lot.

Sarah blushed, feeling weird talking to her dad about such personal things. "Not long. It was kind of an instantaneous thing," she said looking out the window.

Race looked over at her and decided to drop it. "The reason I wanted you to ride with me is because I wanted you to know that you're in danger. My sources at the court told me that Mason's lawyer went in and talked to the judge in a private conference. Ten minutes later, the man was paying Mason's bail. No hearing, no nothing. Completely illegal. The District Attorney is throwing a fit. The guy acting as Mason's attorney is no attorney. He's a witch and a very evil one. He went dark a long time ago and he has the power to manipulate people," Race muttered with loathing.

Sarah felt cold and open as they drove down the street. "He wouldn't happen to be tall, blond and icky would he?" she asked, already knowing the answer.

Race whipped his head around to look at her. "Tell me right now if he's talked to you Sarah," he demanded, pulling the car to the side of the road and turning to stare at her, his green eyes blazing.

Sarah shook her head. "*No*, he didn't talk to me. I didn't give him the chance. I saw him this morning when I was by myself. He was driving by in a car, saw me and then pulled his car over to the side, got out and acted like he was going to follow me. I felt so . . . *cold*. It felt like this cold stream of water was pouring through me and I knew he was dangerous. I could feel my power tripping the nearer he got. He didn't say anything to me but my first instinct was to run

175

as fast as I could to get away from him and so I ran off and got caught up in a group of kids walking to school," she said, watching her father's face turn hard and his eyes deadly.

"His name is Charles Langford. He killed your mother and he would have gladly killed me. He was trying to force me to join his little association and he wasn't shy about threatening you to do it. He thinks he can control politics through our powers. He doesn't care who he hurts or even kills. He'll use any leverage he can to get what he wants. Right now, I think he wants you. I still haven't figured out his connection to Mason, but I'll find out. In the meantime, we're pulling you out of school and we're going on vacation," he said grimly, pulling back into the traffic and heading back towards the Noble Barn.

Sarah's chest hurt as she breathed in and out, trying to accept this new horrible development.

"But what about Mason's trial? Just because he's out on bail, doesn't mean he can just go free. He's going to stand trial for Jill's murder. He can't just get away with it."

Race laughed a low ugly sound that felt harsh. "It took him only 10 minutes to get Mason free. He can control people Sarah. He tried to control me. I fought him off and barely survived. A regular person has no chance. Mason's free. We have to assume he's going to stay that way."

Sarah wrapped her arms around her stomach and remembered how happy she had been that morning. Life changed too fast.

"I'm positive it was Charles who tried to break Agnes' mind. You fixed it of course, but the fact that he can destroy people's minds with a snap of his fingers, shows you what he's capable of. He found out about Drake and your aunt. Drake was stupid and went on a chat group for witches. Charles caught wind of you and found out you were my daughter and got here as fast as he could. I think you're the main goal here Sarah. Charles is just setting up all his players in order to check mate you into doing what it is he wants you to do. Gretchen told me of the dreams she's had about you. I'm worried that things are going to get worse before we're done with this."

Sarah shivered at her father's words and felt the last drop of happiness evaporate. *There went normal. Again.*

Before Race got out of the car, Sarah held up her hand. "Wait, why are you telling just me all this? Shouldn't everyone know?"

Race turned toward his daughter and looked down at his hands. "They will. I just didn't want to spring it on you. You've had enough bad surprises lately. I wanted to tell you privately," he said sounding as if he cared.

Sarah looked down at her hands, surprised to feel the energy leaping to the tips. Her body already felt like it was in trouble. She glanced around the street before reaching for the door.

"Are we being watched?" she asked, her voice wavering.

Race nodded his head. "Yes. I can't see it, but I can feel that we are. Don't worry too much about it. Right now Charles thinks were focusing on Mason. Before he knows it, you'll be far away from here. Safe."

Sarah got out of the car and shivered as a cold breeze stroked her cheek. She threw up a power field around herself and hurried into the store and straight into Zane's arms. Race didn't know about their telepathy connection. She looked up into Zane's eyes and knew he had felt everything Race had told her.

Zane looked over her head smiling placidly at everyone as he thought very clearly into her mind, *You're not going anywhere without me.*

Sarah shivered and let go of Zane. *Maybe you should get as far away from me as possible. I don't want you hurt*, she thought back.

Zane walked over to the café counter and picked up a muffin. He then looked back at her over his shoulder and shook his head slowly. In her mind she heard the words very clearly. *Over my dead body.*

Sarah sighed hoping it didn't come to that. She walked over to Lash who was standing between Gretchen and Agnes looking ill and tired. "Hey buddy, bad news, huh?"

Lash looked at her quietly for a moment and then nodded his head. "That safe feeling I had today? Long gone."

Gretchen who knew all about Lash and his father's blood lust put an arm around Lash's shoulders and looked grim. "Lash there are things you don't know about my mom and I. Please know that we have certain skills that can protect you against your father. You are as safe here with us as if your father was still in jail. He can't touch you here," she promised.

Agnes winked at Lash and handed him a mug of hot chocolate. "Too true. Mason Crossly is toast if he comes within fifteen feet of you," she swore patting Lash on his shoulder.

Lash smiled and took a sip of the chocolate, but then lifted his head up slowly and stared at Gretchen and Agnes. He then turned to Sarah and raised his eyebrows as surprise dawned on his face.

"*You're witches too*?" he asked in awe.

Gretchen and Agnes looked at each other and then turned and looked at Sarah. Sarah held up her hands defensively. "Hey, I wasn't the one who let the cat out of the bag. When I was trying to protect Lash and myself from Mason, he popped right back up and knew immediately I had certain powers. That's when he went crazy to have my blood. He said he'd tasted witches blood before and that if he had me then he wouldn't need anyone else ever again. He went on and on about how great and powerful our blood was. Lash heard and asked me today if it was true. I didn't feel like lying to him," she said with a shrug of her shoulders, wincing at everyone's grim expressions.

Gretchen shook her head and tried to smile. "All the better then. Lash knows that we really can protect him."

Lash frowned and held up his hand. "One problem. Sarah couldn't stop him. If the cops hadn't come when they did she'd be with him right now or dead. I don't mean to put down your power or doubt you, but my dad is different. The blood he's addicted to makes him stronger and more powerful than just about anybody."

Gretchen frowned and stared at Race over Lash's head. Race nodded and looked pained.

"I guess we're back to plan B then. Race you win. Looks like we're going on vacation. Good thing I just hired an assistant manager this week. She can keep the shop going and hire some help while we're laying low. Our children are too important to gamble with."

Zane moved to the center of the group and held up his hands to get everyone's attention. "Hold it. This is our senior year. I don't want to go anywhere. Sarah and Lash don't either. I think running and hiding is the wrong choice here. What Sarah hasn't mentioned and Lash is unaware of, is that I *can* handle Mason. Lash was knocked cold by the time I got there. Mason's strong, granted, but I'm stronger," he said, his eyes blazing as he looked in all the faces around him.

Lash's mouth fell open. "Him too?"

Sarah let out a nervous giggle and nodded. "Sorry Lash, but you're surrounded."

Gretchen patted Lash on the hand but then moved around the counter to grab her son's shoulders.

"I don't want this to come to a show down in the woods between my son and a psychopath. Besides, you've already done that! You've been lucky twice now Zane. I don't think we should push our luck. Race?" she asked, turning for back up.

Race walked forward into the light and nodded. "Zane, I'm aware that you have strong unique gifts. It's imperative that Charles Langford doesn't find out about that. He's a man that wouldn't hesitate to take you and bend you to his will. He's deadly and we can't underestimate what he's willing to do. He's now working with Mason so our threat has doubled. Don't look at it as running and hiding. Look at it as playing it safe. My grandmother's home in Maine is huge, it's right on the coast and it's in a small town where you three can blend in and finish school. Gretchen, Agnes and I will keep track of Charles and Mason from there."

Zane frowned and shook his head. "What would stop Charles and Mason from going to Maine? I don't get how we'd be safer there."

Race winced and looked at his feet. "Charles and I share the same grandmother. He's my cousin and he hasn't set a foot in Rockland since he was disowned twenty years ago. My grandmother is in her eighties now but she's still one of the most powerful witches I know. She's the only witch Charles would never go up against."

Lash cleared his throat causing everyone to turn and look at him. "I'm the only one here that's not a witch, or um, endowed with psychokinesis or whatever," he said, slanting a quick smile at Sarah. "You guys don't even know me. Sarah is the only one here who does. Are you really inviting me to go with you to live in Maine?" he asked, sounding almost pathetically hopeful.

Gretchen walked over and hugged him tightly. "Sweetie, of course you're coming. We couldn't leave you at the mercy of your father. What would that say about us?"

Agnes walked up and lifted Lash's chin so they were looking eye to eye. Lash's eyes widened slightly at the contact. "Lash the first thing you need to know about witches is that our purpose on earth is to protect others. That's the only reason we have our gifts is to watch over everyone else. Of course you're coming with us. You belong to us now Lash."

Lash's face went red as Agnes hugged him too. Sarah looked down at her feet and wiped her eyes quickly as she felt the emotions pour off Lash. Relief, shock and hope. Zane's arm went around her shoulders and she felt a soft kiss on her head and the words, *You are such a softie*, slip through her mind.

Sarah sniffed and looked up to find her father watching her. But something else was watching her too. She glanced behind her at the shop window and shivered.

Sarah looked back at her dad, "How do we leave if we're being watched? I can feel them watching us. How will they not know?"

Gretchen frowned and looked anxiously at her mother. Zane's arms wrapped around Sarah protectively and Lash turned to look out the front windows of the store at the people walking past.

Race sighed but looked determined. "We're leaving in twenty minutes. We leave everything here in Huntingdon. We drive through the night and we don't stop until we're in Maine. I know this will be hard. Once we get there Gretchen, you can make your phone calls to your assistant manager. I'll have a man I know take care of our homes while we're gone. Mason and Charles will go through them I'm sure, but they'll be watched over."

Gretchen looked ill and shook her head. "Mason and Charles don't even know about me or Zane or my mother. Maybe you should take Sarah and Lash and we should stay," she said uneasily.

Race walked over to Gretchen and grasped her arms. "He knows everything about you Gretchen. You're not safe here. I won't be able to help you if you don't come with me," he said, almost tenderly.

Sarah's eyebrows rose up and she turned to look up at Zane who also looked surprised. *Weird.* Floated through her mind.

Agnes stepped forward after Race stepped back and looked into her daughter's eyes. "Gretchen, I can't remember anything about the month prior to my loss of memory. But the nightmares I keep having night after night are about a tall blond man coming to my house and barging through my door. I think Charles Langford is the one who hurt me. We don't have a choice Gretchen. Let's go. If we don't, Sarah will be the one to pay the price," she whispered fiercely.

Every eye in the room turned and locked on Sarah. At Agnes' words, a cold shiver ripped down her spine and even the warmth from Zane standing behind her couldn't ward off the chill.

"*Me?* What do you mean Agnes?"

Race looked fierce and angry. "I didn't want her to know Agnes."

Sarah glared at her father. "I'm eighteen years old and you don't have the right to make that kind of decision for me. If something concerns me then I need to know."

Race glared right back at her. "I'm your father, I have every right to do what I think is best for you."

Sarah felt a rage she didn't know existed, bloom outward and towards her father. "You gave up that right when you put me in the arms of my aunt."

Race stepped back from her and held up a hand. "Control the energy Sarah. Calm down before someone gets hurt. Like me," he said in a calm voice.

Sarah breathed in and out slowly and looked down at her fingers. They were starting to glow. "Sorry. But what I said is true. Agnes, what did you mean by that? Why would I be the one to pay a price?" she asked, ignoring her father and stepping closer to Agnes.

Agnes looked back and forth between her and Race and then shook her head in exasperation. "She's right Race. She needs to know. Sarah, I've been having dreams about you for the last year. They've been getting clearer and stronger. In my dreams, you're being taken to a dark room and when you get there, you're surrounded by candle light and people. You start screaming and that's when they all reach out and grab onto you and the room erupts in lightening. After the power melts down, there's a tall blond man standing over your body and he's smiling like he just won the lottery and he's glowing with power. Your power."

Race pounded his fist on the counter, making Gretchen gasp and everyone else jump. "That's enough Agnes!"

Agnes shook her head at Race and pointed her finger at him. "The dream is a warning. We can stop it Race. Dreams are the power to warn and change. She can't change anything if she doesn't know. Now stop being a fool and think logically. This man, Charles, I still don't know why he harmed me, but I assume it's in connection to Sarah. We're all connected here. We don't have all the pieces yet, but until we do, let's move forward. I say we go now before it's too late," she said, looking each one of them in the face.

Race nodded his head in agreement although he still looked furious. "Let's move. Gretchen, keep the lights on as if we're just going our separate ways. I'll go out the front with Sarah and Lash. Gretchen, you Agnes and Zane slip out the back. Drive as if you're going home but then turn at Patton Avenue and meet me at the freeway exit."

Zane grabbed onto Sarah's arm before she could move. "No. Sarah's coming with me in my Jeep. The more cars to follow the less likely they'll be able to figure out what we're doing. Besides, I'm the only one here who can protect her from Mason. She's not going anywhere without me," he said in a firm, low voice.

Race narrowed his eyes at Zane and shook his head. "Just because I haven't bragged about my powers doesn't mean that I'm not completely able to protect my daughter. You might be able to handle Mason, but don't kid yourself thinking you're a match for Charles. She's safer with me."

Sarah looked back and forth between her father and Zane and felt the tension in the room escalate. She felt a strange new power coming from Zane and knew he wasn't going to back down.

"Race, whatever Zane can't handle I can. We'll be just fine. I'll leave with him and we'll stop and get a pizza like we're on a date. You take Lash and head towards the police station and then keep going. We'll all meet at the freeway exit in 15 minutes. No more arguing, let's just go. *Now*," she said, feeling a coldness creep up her legs. They were running out of time. They had to hurry.

Race gritted his teeth and shook his head. "I don't have time to argue about this. Fine, have it your way, but if anything happens to you Sarah, I won't be able to do anything about it and I'll hold you responsible Zane."

Zane ignored that and pulled Sarah through the store, opening the door with his mind and walking with her out onto the sidewalk.

"You know, your dad is starting to get on my nerves." Zane said in a conversational voice as he opened the door to his jeep for her.

Sarah smiled in a carefree way in case someone was watching her, which she suspected strongly they were. "Join the crowd. He's gone from a complete stranger to a controlling father in the space of a week."

Zane laughed as he glanced up and down the street. He joined her in the jeep and they headed towards the middle of town. "Do you mind if we grab a few burritos in a drive through instead? I don't think we have time for pizza."

Sarah nodded. "You're right. I was just craving pizza, I wasn't thinking."

As they waited in line at the drive through, Sarah turned her body to look around them at the cars and people. "I can't see anyone watching us, so why do I feel it so strongly?" she asked Zane as he reached out to grab her hand.

"I feel it too. Everyone besides Lash was feeling it. Witches are good at premonitions. It's our built in defense mechanism. The sooner we're gone the better."

Zane paid for the food and they drove slowly out of the parking lot and onto Main Street. Zane smiled at her. "The adventure begins."

Sarah smiled back and then leaned over and kissed him quickly. "Thanks for making sure I was with you. I can relax even with life being crazy when you're near me."

Zane stopped smiling and kissed her hand. "There's no way I was letting you out of my sight. I can still see Mason coming for you and hear the things he was saying. They'll have to get through me first to get to you and that's just not going to happen."

Sarah felt instant comfort at his words and relaxed even further into her seat. "I can't believe we're moving to Maine. I've lived in Pennsylvania my whole life," she said, shaking her head as she unwrapped her burrito.

Zane grinned and pushed his jeep to 75 mph as he hit the long stretch of road between town and the freeway exit. "I'm already picturing romantic camp fires on the shore, looking at the stars and eating lobster and crab until I'm full."

Sarah laughed, wishing she hadn't just spilled hot sauce on the only jeans to her name. "Yeah, with you, me, Lash, my father, your mother and your grandmother, I wonder if we'll even have a moment to ourselves now."

Zane winced. "Where there's a will, there's a way. And speaking of crowds, what's going on with your dad and my mom? Did you catch that tender little moment?" he asked irritably.

Sarah had a mouth of burrito and couldn't talk so she spoke with her mind. *Looks like you might have a step-dad soon. I hear he's a lot of fun.*

Zane shook his head at her and slowed down at the turn off. They were the first one's there. He turned the car off and locked the doors, turning in his seat to see the cars coming from behind. "So in that scenario you and I would be step-brother and sister."

Sarah made a face. "That's kind of gross and possibly illegal. I guess I better start dating Lash instead."

Zane turned and stared at her with a raised eyebrow, not looking amused at all.

Sarah grinned. "Relax, after what you said today in school, I've come to the decision that I think you're right. I do believe you and I are kind of meant to be. Step-siblings or not," she said and leaned over to kiss him.

Zane shook his head at her but reached over and put his hand behind her neck as he kissed her back. The honk behind them had them pulling apart quickly and staring hard at the car pulling in behind them. It was Race and Lash.

Race hopped out of his car and jogged to Zane's window. "Where's your mom? She should have been here by now."

Zane frowned and took his cellphone out. "I'll call her."

185

Race and Sarah stared at Zane as they listened to the ring turn into a message. Zane ended the call and slipped his phone back into his pocket.

"She'll be here. She might have stopped at the house to get makeup or my grandmother's medicine or something."

Race looked at the road with agitation coming off him in waves. "I'm worried. I'm going back," he said and ran back to his car.

Zane opened the jeep door to go after Race when a strange tan car none of them recognized pulled up beside them. Sarah hopped out of the jeep in case it was trouble. She ran around to Zane's side as Gretchen and Agnes stepped out.

Race ran to Gretchen's side, grabbing her hand. "What happened? Where'd you get this car?" he demanded.

Gretchen smiled weakly. "This is my father's car. It's been sitting in the garage for over a decade. I had to jump it to get it to start, but its working fine. I stopped by the house to get my mom's heart medicine and when we got back to the car, all of my tires were flat. Race, I think they know."

Zane and Race stared down the road as Lash came to stand by Sarah's side. Sarah glanced at Lash and tried to smile in a reassuring way. Lash grimaced and shoved his hands in his pockets, looking worried.

"Let's go. Right now," Race ordered. They all hurried back to their separate vehicles and were on the freeway within minutes.

Sarah turned, staring at Gretchen's car behind them and the empty road going back to town.

"Do you really think they know?" Sarah asked, leaning her head against the leather seat.

Zane glanced at her and then pushed his jeep up to 80. "Yeah, I do. But if popping my mom's tires is all he did, then they were still caught off guard. I don't think they were expecting us to make a run for it. I don't think they'll follow us Sarah. Besides the further I get away from town, the easier I feel. That heavy feeling of being watched is almost completely gone. What about you?" he asked, glancing in his rear view mirror.

Sarah breathed a sigh of relief and nodded. "Yeah, it's fading fast. I think you're right. So how far is it to Maine?" she asked as she turned the radio on.

Zane grimaced and reached for the last burrito. "It's about six hours from here. But I don't know where in Maine, Rockland is. Maine has a very long coast line. It could take us a very long time to get there if it's by the Canadian border."

Sarah grimaced. "Maybe when we stop for gas I can get a magazine or something. We'll have to switch off so you can rest too. Don't worry though. I'm a good driver."

Zane frowned as he realized she was right. "Do you even have your license?"

Sarah grinned and shook her head. "Nope. My aunt was holding it over my head. She wouldn't allow me to get one until I agreed to her little ceremony."

Zane groaned and caressed the dashboard. "You know I love this jeep, don't you?"

Sarah laughed and repositioned her seat to a more comfortable angle. "And to think you insisted on the two of us driving together. This might actually be fun."

Zane reached over and tickled her, making her scream and giggle. "Stop Zane! I swear I'll zap you," she warned playfully.

Zane winced and sat back. They talked for the next three hours until Race signaled a stop at the next gas station. They all poured out of the cars for bathroom breaks, snacks and magazines.

Race motioned for everyone to gather around before they jumped back in their cars. "We've got quite a way to go still. I think if they were going to try something, they would have by now. But let's not get careless. Keep alert and be watchful. Honk your horn if anything strange or out of the ordinary happens. If your car stops working or a tire pops, it could be them. I say we punch up the speed a little too. The sooner we get there, the better."

"Where in Maine is this town? How many more hours are we driving?" she asked, looking at the jeep and wishing they could stop for a night in a hotel.

Race looked at the group. "It's past Portland and Brunswick. You've got about a good five hours left. Let's go."

Sarah and Zane hopped back in the jeep and were the first ones out on the road. Sarah groaned as she clicked her seat belt. "Five more hours? *Ugh*."

Zane shook his head. "Not exactly how I pictured spending the evening when I woke up this morning."

Sarah laughed and grabbed Zane's hand. "That's an understatement."

Their caravan drove the next five hours peacefully, with no disturbances. They had a bad moment when Gretchen honked her horn but that had turned out to be a false alarm. Agnes had to take a bathroom break. At 3 in the morning, they followed Race's car up a long driveway that led to a pitch black home. It was a dark night and no lights were on in the house. It was so dark, Sarah couldn't even tell what the house looked like. Race ran back to the jeep after getting out of the car.

"I didn't call my grandmother and warn her we were coming. This might take a minute. Sit tight."

Zane sighed and rolled his window up again. "Get ready to sleep in the jeep," he said sounding exhausted.

Sarah groaned, already knowing the seats didn't recline all the way back. She was so sore and tired she could cry. She watched her father walk up the steps of the porch and pound on the door. A few moments later, the door opened and Race walked in, shutting the door behind him.

Sarah looked at Zane, but he had fallen asleep, his head tilted to the side. She leaned forward as a couple lights went on in the front room. She turned and looked back at Gretchen's car, but it was dark and silent. Ten very long minutes later, Race opened the door and ran lightly down the steps. He paused and said something to Lash through the window and then came to her side of the car. She rolled down her window for him.

"She knew we were coming, so everything's ready. Let's go in and get some sleep. We'll talk about everything tomorrow," he said and then stood up to go to Gretchen.

"Wait. If she was ready, what took you so long? You were in there for a while."

Race looked away and then back at her. "My grandmother wanted to make some rules clear. We had a discussion and have come to an agreement. We'll talk it all over tomorrow Sarah. Just know that everything's okay now. You'll be safe here," he promised and then walked away.

Sarah sighed, wishing her father was more forthcoming with information. "Zane. *Zane!* Wake up. Let's go in and get some sleep," she said, shaking his arm.

Zane's head tilted up and he stared at her groggily. "We can go in?" he asked.

Sarah nodded and opened her door, rubbing her arms vigorously. It was freezing here. And all she had was a light hoody. She ran up the stairs and stood in the shadows waiting for everyone else to make their way to the house.

"You're not what I expected."

Sarah jumped and whipped her head around. An old woman, dressed in a long nightgown and bathrobe stood staring at her from the doorway. She had shoulder length white hair and light green eyes. Sarah realized she was looking at her great-grandmother.

"What were you expecting?" she asked curiously.

The woman stepped closer and reached out a finger to touch her arm. Electrical sparks erupted where her finger touched her and Sarah immediately moved back, frowning at the woman.

"You're a strong one. From my dreams, I thought you'd be weak and helpless. You're not. You're just as strong as they are. You've got a chance to survive after all," she said sounding surprised.

Sarah frowned and stepped back into Zane's chest, knowing he'd be there.

"What do you mean she has a chance to survive after all?" Zane demanded putting an arm around her shoulders.

The woman stepped close to Zane and touched his arm too. Sparks didn't erupt, but she pulled her finger back sharply as if she'd been cut.

"So that's what I was missing. This changes everything. Oh I'm so relieved. Come in, come in everyone. You are most welcome to my home. My companion Beatrice will show you to your rooms. Come, come, before the night wants to join us," she said, shooing them inside imperiously.

Zane leaned down and whispered into her ear. "Your grandma is interesting."

Sarah sighed tiredly and followed the woman inside where the large two story entrance way was dimly lit. A small woman in her fifties with short curly brown hair and wearing a pink sweat suit stood by the staircase smiling.

"Frannie can't do the stairs anymore so I'll show you all up. Come this way, you must be exhausted," she said kindly and motioned with her arm to follow her.

Gretchen and Agnes walked past her, taking her arms in theirs creating a united front. They walked up the stairs silently, too tired to say anything. Beatrice gestured to the first room and pointed to Gretchen and Agnes.

"This will be your room. There are two beds and you'll have your own bath. Sarah, you'll be right next door. You have your room all to yourself. It's small, but you have your own bath too. And if you ask me, you have the best view of the ocean. Men, follow me. You're just down here," she said and walked down the hallway, turning on lights as she went.

Zane leaned down and kissed her cheek before walking away. *Good night beautiful,* he whispered in her mind.

She sighed and walked into her new room. She turned on the lights and looked around. Pale, butter cream walls, way too much lace and a window seat. She smiled faintly and then found her bed, collapsing on it. She'd appreciate the handmade quilt tomorrow. She thought the word *off* and closed her eyes as the lights above turned off. She fell into a deep, fog-filled dream and didn't stir as a woman walked into her room, uninvited and gently laid another blanket on top of her. As she reached down to touch Sarah's hair, she jerked her hand back, gasping at the sudden pain along her nerve endings. She hissed in pain and then slowly walked out of the room and down the hallway with a triumphant smile on her wrinkled face.

Chapter 20 - Fate Changer

Sarah woke up feeling refreshed and energized. She sat up in bed and stretched her hands high above her head. She glanced around her room and smiled at the bright cheery room. It was so feminine and completely unlike her, but yet at the same time, it made her happy. She had no idea why. She moved to get out of bed and noticed for the first time some clothes laid out at the foot of her bed. She reached over and pulled brown striped leggings, a dark brown, short corduroy skirt and a light tan silky sweater. She leaned over the bed and saw the knee high, dark brown leather boots. Her eyebrows went up as she wondered who had bought all of this for her and how in the world they knew her size.

She lifted the skirt and sweater and saw that underclothes had been placed there for her as well. Thoughtful, but kind of weird too. She hopped out of bed and walked into the bathroom, smiling at all the white tile and chrome. The skylight above let in natural light and she didn't even need to turn on the light to see everything. She turned on the shower and sighed in pure happiness as steam enveloped the room. After her shower she wrapped herself in a long, luxurious white towel and walked over to the vanity. Make-up in all the forms and colors she loved were laid out just waiting for her, along with perfume, combs, brushes and a hair dryer.

It was too good to be true. She grabbed her favorite brand of leave in hair conditioner and poured some in her hands running it through her wavy damp hair. She decided to let it air dry while she got dressed and put on makeup. Today was a new day. She had a new home, new boyfriend, new father and friends and now new clothes and make up. Life was starting to look up again. After flipping her hair over and shaking her waves out with her fingers, she stood back up and then walked over to the floor to ceiling mirror. No one was there to make fun of her so she gave in to a girly impulse and twirled around. She had never been one to be vain, but as she stared at her reflection in the mirror she had to admit she looked better than she ever had before, as if she'd just stepped out of a teen magazine. She grinned at herself fleetingly and hurried out of her room and down the stairs to find everyone.

She followed the voices to a dining room at the back of the house with large windows facing the ocean. The gray and stormy seascape was breathtaking, dangerous and beautiful all at the same time. She stared, enraptured at the tumultuous scene, barely noticing when Zane and Lash came to stand beside her.

"You look *amaaaaazing*," Lash said, drawing the word out in a way that drew her attention to him and had her blushing. She blinked at the blatant appreciation in his voice and punched him lightly in the arm.

"Thanks Lash," she said easing away from him.

He reached out a hand to stop her though. "You should always wear leather boots," he whispered with a wink and then turned to sit down with a grin on his face as Zane stared at him warningly.

Sarah laughed, embarrassed by the attention and looked up at Zane. She blinked in surprise and noticed he had been given a makeover too. Gone were the skater clothes, the plaid button downs over t-shirts and jeans that he always wore and instead he was wearing a form-fitting cream cashmere sweater and jeans. He looked incredible.

"We match," she said, grinning up into his face.

Zane slipped an arm around her waist and pulled her close. "If I wasn't already in love with you, I would be now. Who could resist you looking like this?" he asked for her ears only and leaned in for a quick kiss.

Sarah opened her eyes in surprise and cleared her throat, embarrassed that they had an audience. *Zane!* she sent to his mind, in a stern rebuke.

He laughed at her and then pulled her by the hand to the table, laden with plates of bacon, sausage, eggs, hash browns and pancakes. Sarah's stomach growled faintly and she took a seat by Gretchen.

"This looks incredible," she said.

Race handed her a plate. "You look pretty today Sarah," he said, almost shyly.

Sarah blinked in surprise that her father would make such a personal comment.

"Oh, um, *thanks*. Who gave me these clothes do you know? They were just lying on my bed when I woke up," she asked, looking around the table and noticing that everyone was wearing new clothes and looking good. Gretchen was wearing a long denim skirt, dark brown boots and a white fitted shirt with a black scarf looped loosely around her neck. Agnes was wearing a pale green cashmere sweater, suede tan pants and leather shoes. Her father was wearing dark jeans and a white button down shirt, looking relaxed, stylish and attractive. She glanced at Gretchen and could tell she thought so too. And then there was Lash. He was dressed all in black. Black jeans, black boots, and a black silk t-shirt hanging around his hips. She saw a black leather jacket hanging from the back of his chair and grinned at him. He was loving it.

"You can thank your grandmother. I asked her the same thing this morning and she told me she's known we were coming for months. She said she had a lot of fun picking everything out. She's quite the internet shopper."

Race sat across from Gretchen and smiled at her. Lash handed him the platter of bacon and everyone got down to the business of eating.

Agnes was the one who broke the silence. "So what now Race? We can't just wander around this old house, looking like models out of a *Visit Maine* brochure. What are we going to do?"

Race glanced at Gretchen first before answering. "Simple. I'm going to get Zane, Sarah and Lash registered down at the high school. You and Gretchen are going to be on the phone

194

most of the day to employees and suppliers to get your book store taken care of. Me? I'm going to be busy opening my up my natural healing clinic in town. From now on, it's life as usual. At least as close to it as we can make it. I have a house of my own closer to town. I'll be moving there in a few days after I get cleaners there and get it stocked. Gretchen, you, Sarah and Agnes will be staying here with my grandmother and the boys will move in with me. I don't think it's appropriate to have two teenage boys and a pretty teenage girl in the same house," he said looking at Zane and Lash with narrowed eyes.

Lash looked disappointed, but Zane looked grim. "I'm not leaving Sarah here unprotected. I don't care what you say. Where she is, *I am*," he stated coldly, staring Race down.

"Young man, you just simmer down. I can protect her just as good if not better than you. You can watch over her when she's not under this roof," said a light feminine voice from behind them.

Everyone turned and looked at the petite, thin woman who stood before them. She was wearing an expensive looking, pale pink leisure suit that Sarah had sworn she'd seen Mariah Carey wearing last week. She looked kind of fierce.

"No offense ma'am, but I know what I'm up against and I'm not taking any chances with her."

Sarah reached a foot over to touch Zane's and he reached out and took her hand under the table. She felt her anxiety lessen immediately.

"Young man, you don't have the slightest clue what you're up against. I can see that you doubt my talents," she said wonderingly.

Race stood up and shook his head at his grandmother. "Grandmother, *please*. Now is not the time or place."

The woman held her hand up and then pointed out the window at the ocean. A wave rose up out of the choppy sea and hurled itself onto the beach. Everyone stared, with wide, surprised eyes as the water reared up and turned into a pale, water dragon before throwing itself back into the ocean.

Zane stared out the window for a while before turning to look at the small woman. *"Holy crap.* I cannot believe you just did that."

The woman smiled at him with a twinkle in her eyes. "Don't judge people based on their outward appearance kid. Now that's settled. Let me introduce myself to everyone. You lot were too tired last night to care, but my name is Francis Livingston your hostess for the foreseeable future. Now I've seen you in my head for months, but it's so nice to see you in person. I'm glad all the clothes fit. You young man, are going to break hearts. I'm keeping my eye on you," she said sternly, looking at Lash.

Lash grinned at her and winked before taking another bite of eggs. Francis laughed and glanced around the room.

"So you're the pretty lady that has stolen my grandson's heart. I can see why. You're just as beautiful on the inside as you are on the outside. Perfect. And you Miss Agnes. You and I will be good friends. I've seen it. We have a lot in common. And you two," she said, turning to stare at Sarah and Zane.

Zane and Sarah glanced at each other, smiling but feeling awkward too.

"You're the crux of the matter aren't you? Sarah you are safe here for as long as I want you to be. This is my town and Charles knows better than to set foot inside my lines. I don't know why he's so focused on you but he's determined to have you. Too bad, is what I say. He's going to have to learn to live with disappointment. But until then, I have much to teach you. You haven't been taught a blessed thing about who you are or what you can do. I blame your father for that. But that's going to change here and now. And you Zane Miner. You're a special one you are. I didn't understand at first but I can see it now. The moment I touched you I knew why you'd come. You're the fate changer."

Francis smiled almost gleefully at Zane and then turned to take in the table of people looking at her. "Evil isn't going to know what's coming."

Sarah watched as the seemingly frail woman sat down across from her and started heaping large portions of food on her plate. She studied the woman carefully as conversations picked up around her.

You better eat girl, you're going to need your strength, a voice whispered through her mind.

She gasped and looked at Zane, but he was busy eating his eggs and pouring orange juice. She turned her head and looked back at her grandmother who was looking right at her. Francis smiled and winked. *You've got a lot of surprises in store honey.*

Sneak Peak at Blood Rush Book #2 in The Lost Witch Trilogy

Chapter 1 - Premonition

Francis Livingston pulled her sweater tighter around herself as she stared broodingly out across the ocean. Standing on the widow's walk of her home always centered her and brought her peace. But not today. Too much had happened and so much was getting ready to happen. Rockland Maine had been free from Charles Langford for almost eighteen years. Her lines of protection were strong but she had no idea if she could truly keep him out. From the news she gathered from other witches around the world, Charles had been busy gaining more and more power over the years and by means too evil to comprehend. He'd broken his own family to gain what he wanted and had killed them in the process. He had no morals, no compassion and no heart. His only motive in life was to destroy, to take and to own. And now he wanted Sarah.

"Sarah is so much stronger than I imagined, so why do I feel so uneasy Bea? Something's wrong. I feel danger, but I can't see it. Tell me what I'm missing," she demanded.

Beatrice ran a hand through her short brown waves and leaned against the wooden railing of the widow's walk. "Frannie, you're always seeing shadows that aren't there. Just last month you said a huge disaster was about to take place and the only bad thing that happened was Conrad Gaminski asked me out on a date."

Francis snorted and shook her head at her friend. "Perspective Bea. Last month, Charles made contact with Sarah's aunt Lena and made plans to attain her. I would call that disastrous."

Bea winced and sighed heavily. "Speaking of Sarah and all the others, are you up to this? You've been on your own for a long time and now you've got a house full of strangers. Are you really going to teach her?"

Francis frowned into the wind and tightened her hands on the wood railing. "He's coming for her Bea. I can't let him take her power, her essence. If I stand back and do nothing now, I'm just as guilty as if I gift wrapped her and handed her to him. She needs to be prepared. I'm getting older every second and someday soon, Charles will be able to walk through this town just like he did eighteen years ago. You better believe I'll teach her."

Beatrice rubbed her friend's back comfortingly. "He'll back off now that he knows she's under you protection. He'll focus on someone or something else."

Francis swallowed and shook her head. "He won't back off Bea. I can feel it. The only thing that gives me hope is that boy they brought with them. Zane. Now we have a real chance."

Beatrice clucked comfortingly and took Francis' hand in hers. "Let's go inside Frannie. It's getting cold."

Francis let her friend draw her away, but she looked over her shoulder one last time and noticed a lone crow flying slowly in circles over the water. She shuddered as if a blast of cold wind had slapped her. She pulled out of Beatrice's hold and turned to face the ocean again. She stared hard at the ocean and watched as a giant hand of water reached up into the air to grasp the bird. The bird screamed in rage and flew high out of the reach of the water. The hand collapsed back into the dark waves of water as the crow flew out of sight.

Francis felt her heart beating fast and let a shuddering breath out.

"Frannie?"

Francis shook her head and led the way into the house. "We haven't got much time."

Sneak Peak at Book 1 in The Taming The Wolf Trilogy, Werewolf Dreams

Chapter 1 – Summer Vacation

Ava hopped out of her father's army green jeep and stared around the depressing little valley. She pulled her long, wavy dark blond hair back and twisted it into a knot. She winced at what she saw. Nothing but trees, abandoned vacation cottages and a small lake. If there was ever a setting for a horror movie, this was it. This was how she was going to spend her last summer before college? Ugh. She sighed and then smiled quickly as her father glanced at her suspiciously.

"Ava? Something wrong?" he asked.

Harry Paskell didn't look like the typical single father. He looked like he was only about ten years older than her when in fact he was forty-three. He wore a white button up shirt open at the neck with tan cargo shorts. His high tech running shoes were his only nod to his wealth. Everything else screamed poor college student. His dark, golden brown hair waved back from his forehead, showing a handsome, austere face that her friends assured her was gorgeous.

Ava tried to smooth out her features but her dad was on to her. He'd always been able to sense even her slightest changes in mood. It was kind of annoying. Being a teenage girl with a dad who could practically read her mind was awkward to say the least.

"Well, you said that we'd be spending the summer together and helping your friend Tobias investigate a crime. This isn't what I pictured in my head. When you said Canada, I was thinking ski resort. You know, with um . . . people. There's no one here," she said, pointing at the eerily quiet valley.

Harry grimaced and glanced behind him. "It is a little deserted feeling. It's called Wolf Song Lake. It's named for all the wolves that populate this area. I spent a lot of time here as a boy," he said wistfully as he shaded his eyes.

Ava glanced at the lake curiously now. Her father never talked about his childhood or past. Interesting. She glanced around curiously. "Wolf Song Lake. What a pretty name for such a creepy place.

I'd love to see a real wolf in the wild. Remember those dreams I used to have all the time when I was a kid about that beautiful light brown wolf running wild?"

Harry frowned and looked at her piercingly for a moment before smiling. "How could I forget? You had that dream constantly. Your bedroom walls were covered with drawings of wolves."

Ava smiled, remembering her childhood obsession. "Soon taken over by my obsession with soccer. Followed by karate, followed by soft-ball, followed by gymnastics. Yeah, I'd like to move on to socializing for my new hobby if you don't mind."

Harry's eyes warmed and he smiled at her "Don't worry. I know you'll see at least one person today out here. Tobias told me he'd send someone out to meet us and show us around, so I can guarantee you'll be meeting someone soon."

"I'm sure that'll be so exciting," Ava said under her breath picturing an old grizzled mountain man. Harry raised an eyebrow at her sarcasm but ignored her comment.

"I'll be taking samples here but we'll be staying in a town about fifteen miles away. It's where I grew up. There will be plenty of people there. Sort of," he added quietly. "But we'll be so busy here, I don't think there'll be much time to socialize," he said, his eyebrows coming together in a V as if he were suddenly worried.

Ava closed her eyes and counted to ten in search of patience. She got to three and gave up. "It's almost as if you don't want me to socialize. This is my summer before I go to college and you've kept me so busy these last few years that I've never even had a boyfriend. I'm sorry dad, but if there's a town with people, then I want to meet them. I'm going to find the cutest boy there and then I'm going to go on a date," she said, throwing her hands in the air and turning away from her father as she automatically went into emotional control mode.

Ava closed her eyes, gripped her arms and concentrated on breathing slowly as she recited the alphabet backwards. She could feel the blood rushing through her veins begin to slow down gradually. She stopped when she felt her father's hands on her shoulders.

"Ava, I'm sorry. I know that your life has been a little different compared to other girls. I know that you look at all your friends going to dances and dating and you feel cheated and left out. I'm sorry for that. Someday soon, you'll understand why."

Ava opened her eyes and glared at her feet. "I hate that word someday. I've heard it all my life and it's just a carrot that you've held in front of my face to keep me quiet and in the shadows. I'll give you this summer Dad, but then my life is my own. No matter what," she said quietly.

She felt her father step away from her and turned to watch the man who had raised her single handedly since she was three. He had his hands on his hips and he was looking down at his feet with his face in shadow. Ava was so irritated with him she could scream, but she could never deny her love for him. He raised his head finally and she felt her heart soften against her will. He looked so torn, guilty almost.

"Ava, you'll have all the answers you've ever wanted at the end of this summer. For good or bad. Then you'll understand why you've had to live your life the way you have. I've done the best I can Ava. I love you," he said, looking at her with tormented eyes.

Ava shook her head and walked into his arms, hugging him tightly. "I know you have. But it's time I had a little freedom. I love you too, but the cage has to open or I'll go insane," she said softly stepping back.

Harry let his daughter go and nodded. "I know. I was the same way at your age."

Ava smiled and nodded her head. "Good, then you understand how I feel. So I'm warning you. All the cute boys in a fifty mile radius better watch out."

Harry winced and then gave up and laughed. "I'll keep that in mind, but Ava, all the boys your age around here are a little different and not the type of men I want you dating. It's probably wise to wait for college to start socializing. " he said running his hand through his hair.

Ava raised an eyebrow and tilted her head as she studied her father. Sometimes she could sense her father's feelings and right now, she could tell he was honestly worried but was trying to hide it. But why?

"If you didn't want me to socialize with the people who live around here this summer, then why did you insist that I come with you? Kendra invited me to spend the summer with her family at their vacation house in California. I just don't get any of this," she said with a frustrated groan.

Harry held up his hands for peace. "I told you Ava. This is our last summer together before you leave for college and you start your life on your own. There are certain things I need to explain to you and I realized that this was the perfect opportunity. Sometimes showing is better than telling."

Ava let her shoulders drop and she shook her head. "Fine, fine, fine. Let's get on with it then."

Harry's face relaxed into an easy smile. "Exactly what I was thinking. Let's grab our packs and head down to those cottages. I need to take samples and do a little investigating. We'll stop for lunch in a couple hours. Sound good?" he said, opening the back of the jeep and grabbing their back packs. He tossed the light tan pack to her and kept the black one for himself. She slipped her pack on and then watched wide eyed as her father attached a lethal looking gun to a leg holster as if he did that kind of thing every day.

"Uh Dad?" she asked softly, trying to swallow back her unease.

Harry glanced up and grimaced as he saw her reaction. "It's a Beretta Px4 9mm. Just a precaution. The research I've been hired to do is kind of specialized. There were quite a few attacks on tourists here about 6 months ago. The place is totally deserted now, but it's my job to discover what exactly happened here," he said as he grabbed a couple water bottles, throwing one to her.

Ava caught the bottle automatically one handed and nodded. "Not your typical research project, huh?" she murmured, wondering why anyone would hire her father to do something on this scale. Harry Paskell was a geneticist, not a CSI investigator.

Harry glanced at her and grinned as if he could read her mind. "I'm sort of a specialized investigator on this project. Everyone leaves a DNA imprint. Whatever or whoever attacked the tourists will have left their DNA. I'm here to track them down. I owe it to my friends and family to find whoever did this," he said quietly.

Ava blinked in surprise. For a moment, her dad had looked a little dangerous. Weird. "So where's my gun?" she asked jokingly as they walked down the hill towards the lake.

Harry glanced at her and slipped on his sunglasses. "Actually I thought about it, but there wasn't time for you to take a class before we came. If anything happens just use your instincts," he said cryptically.

Ava stared at her father's back in shock. She'd heard nothing but the opposite her entire life. Ava, control your natural impulses. Ava, think logically. Ava, you're different than other kids. You must never lose control.

"So what you're saying is, that whatever attacked those people six months ago, might attack us?" she asked, feeling a little better about their summer now. Kendra would be so jealous when she told her the real reason they were spending the summer in Canada. The beach couldn't compare to mysterious attacks on tourists.

Harry glanced over his shoulder at her and shook his head. "Probably not, but just be on your guard. Listen to what your senses are telling you," he said.

Ava's eyes went round in awe. "And then what? Do a back hand spring? Scare them off with a hand stand or cart wheel?" she asked, grinning at her father's back.

Harry laughed and jumped over a pile of branches lying strewn on the path. "That's not a bad idea. Being a trained gymnast means you're physically strong enough to handle just about anything. But if anything happens, just yell for me and I'll take care of anyone that is a threat."

Ava leaped gracefully over the branches, landing beside her father. "And what if you're too far away?" she asked, just now realizing that they really could be in danger.

Harry gave her a half smile. "Trust me, I'll hear you."

Ava shrugged and walked in silence beside her father. She closed her eyes for a second and let her senses take over. The eerie silence caused a slight shiver to run down her back but she blocked it out. And then she felt it. Someone or something was watching them.

Ava's eyes popped open and she felt a stream of adrenaline start to flow through her veins.

"What's the matter?" Harry asked, looking at her curiously.

Ava glanced around, noticing all the dark shadows hiding behind trees and rocks. "We're being watched. I can feel it," she said softly, still scanning their surroundings.

Harry repositioned his back pack without stopping. "I know. We've been watched since we got here. Don't worry about it. It's probably just an animal."

Ava felt a few hairs at the back of her neck rise up and she stared at a small ravine where a dense amount of fir trees grew. Whatever it was, it was tracking her and her father.

They walked down the path to the first vacation cottage and paused at the steps leading up to the small porch looking out on the lake. Ava turned and stared at the pristine view and wondered what could have scared everyone away from something so beautiful.

"You know we could have brought the jeep right to the front door Dad. Why did we have to hike from the main road?" she asked as her father took off his back pack and opened the zipper.

Harry grabbed some plastic gloves, tweezers and baggies before answering. "It's still basically a crime scene. I don't want to disturb any prints," he said, glancing around the cottage and lake, pausing on the trees that nestled around the small house protectively.

Ava moved to follow her father but he held up hand. "You stay here. I'll let you know when or if I need you to take pictures," he said and then disappeared into the cottage not waiting for her response.

Ava huffed out a breath and then rolled her eyes. Knowing her father, he could be inside for hours and not remember she was waiting. She slipped off her back pack and rooted around inside until she found a granola bar. She walked over to the lake and sat down on an old Adirondack chair and stared at the silent, smooth water as she finished her snack. She glanced at her watch and then sighed.

She knew back home in Bellevue Washington, her friends were going off to their jobs at the mall and spending their free time sailing and going dancing. Having fun. She understood her father not wanting her to stay home all summer by herself, that's why she'd been so certain her father would have agreed to let her go with Kendra down to California for at least a month. Being told no had come as a complete shock. The only reason she wasn't throwing a fit was because deep down, she did want to spend more time with her father. They'd both been so busy with their separate lives lately it had felt like they were slowly growing apart. She had school and sports and he had his classes to teach and his research. But hanging out in front of creepy crime scenes was not what she would call a good bonding experience.

She ran her hands through her long golden hair and then paused. She felt like she was being watched again. She turned and scanned her surroundings with a glare. Nothing. Not even the sound of birds. She blinked as she realized that the quietness surrounding her wasn't exactly natural. It was too quiet. Where had all the animals gone? She shivered unexpectedly and then smiled at herself. She,

Kendra and their other friend Larissa loved going to scary movies on the weekends. Her imagination had always been over the top and now she was doing a good job of freaking herself out.

She was just restless after the long ride in the jeep. She needed to be at a gym. If she could work out, she'd be able to get rid of the excess adrenaline she always seemed to have too much of. She stood up and stretched and then walked over to the beach. She glanced around the shoreline and smiled at the soft sand. Perfect. She would just work out here. Who needed a mat when she had sand?

Ava stretched out and warmed up her muscles before jumping into a sprint and jumping up to twist her body into a triple full layout with three twists. She landed on her feet and laughed happily.

This is what she loved the most. Doing what she loved doing without an audience. It was so much more fun to fly through the air when no one was critiquing every move she made. Ava turned and glanced at the silent cottage her father was working in and shrugged. No one to see but the trees. She grinned and jumped into another sprint and then threw her body higher than she ever had before, fueled by freedom and the joy of having complete control over every muscle.

She landed perfectly on her feet and then bent backwards, creating a flawless back bend before kicking her feet up into the air. She walked around the soft sand on her hands and then got bored, so she balanced on one hand as she brought the other close to her side.

"How long can you hold that?"

Ava squeaked and flipped quickly to her feet, frowning because not one sense had warned her that someone had casually walked up to her.

She stood up and stared at the man standing in front of her, looking at her speculatively. He was tall, probably as tall as her dad and he had glossy medium brown hair that hung just below his ears and bright clear, light blue eyes. She couldn't tell how old he was, but he looked a little older than her. She looked him up and down quickly and recognized his strength and power immediately. What was he? A professional athlete? But there was one thing she did know for certain. He was absolutely the most stunning man she'd ever met in her life.

She pushed her long dark blond hair out of her light brown eyes and frowned at the man. "I thought I was alone," she said, sounding as irritated as she felt.

The man grinned at her and shrugged. "I would have said hello before but then I would have missed the show. I'm Cyrus Carlston and you must be Harry Paskell's research assistant," he said holding his hand out to her.

Ava relaxed and smiled back. Cyrus Carlston must be the guide her father had mentioned. "I'm Ava, Harry's daughter. It's nice to meet you," she said reaching out to grasp the man's firm hard hand.

Cyrus looked surprised and he stared at her curiously, not letting go of her hand as he studied her face carefully.

"Harry's daughter? Interesting," he said softly, still holding her hand. He stepped closer to her, leaning down as if he were trying to see inside of her.

Ava lost her smile as she stared up into his ice blue eyes. This guy had no clue about personal space. She pulled on her hand, but he refused to let go.

"Are you going to let go of my hand now, or are you going to tell me my future?" she asked, jerking hard one more time on her hand forcing Cyrus to let go.

Cyrus looked down at his now empty hand and frowned at her, before his face cleared and he smiled.

"I see a summer filled with excitement and nights filled with mystery and romance," he said with a grin before stepping back and shoving his hands into his jeans pockets.

Ava laughed and rolled her eyes as she glanced at the cottage. "With my dad watching every move I make? Yeah, right."

Cyrus glanced at the cottage and stared at the door as a second later it opened and her father walked out.

"There you are. I was wondering when you were going to show up," Harry called out as he ran lightly down the pathway to the beach.

Ava smiled in surprise. Sometimes she forgot just how fast her father could move when he wanted to. Within seconds he was shaking Cyrus's hand and looking at her quickly with a warning in his eyes.

Ava moved back from Cyrus and stood next to her father as she studied the man who was still looking right at her.

"Harry, you never told my father that you had a daughter. How old is Ava? Eighteen, nineteen?" he asked, his eyes bright with curiosity.

Harry waited until Cyrus looked back at him before answering. Harry's eyes had narrowed to slits and his shoulders seemed larger somehow as he stepped closer to Cyrus. "Ava is eighteen and my having a daughter is nobody's business but my own. By birth she belongs to no one but herself. She's half. She's of no interest to anyone. Especially you," he said, his voice sounding like hot metal, dangerous and violent.

Ava's mouth fell open in surprise. Her father sounded like he was almost threatening Cyrus. But why? And what the heck did he mean by her being half? Half Canadian? Like that was a big deal.

Cyrus's welcoming smile stayed in place as he looked at her again and she felt a little zip of adrenaline flicker down her arms. "I might disagree with you. My father wants to give you the files himself tonight after dinner but he wanted me to show you the sight of the last attack since it's the freshest. Follow me," he said and then walked past them and down the shoreline.

Ava looked at her father silently, waiting for some kind of explanation. Harry stared at her for a moment before walking to her and grasping her shoulders in his strong hands. "Cyrus isn't the type of man you're used to being around. You should never be alone with him," he said quietly, glancing at Cyrus.

Ava frowned. "Why? Is he dangerous?" she whispered back staring in sudden fear at Cyrus.

Harry closed his eyes for a moment and then shook his head. "No, not in the way you're thinking. Ava, you're a beautiful young woman and you're innocent. I've made sure of that. There are men who would take advantage of that and of the fact that you're, well . . . different. Be on your guard," he said and then hurried after Cyrus, catching up within seconds.

Ava huffed out a breath and ran back to get her back pack before following her father. She'd felt different her whole life and she was sick to death of it. She wondered sadly if there was anywhere in the world where she could fit in.

Acknowledgements

There are many people I'd like to thank who helped me along my way. I'd like to thank Zach Hill for editing and Jessica G. for her feedback. I also want to thank LFD Designs for Authors for the amazing covers they came up with for The Lost Witch Trilogy. Love them. I also want to thank my kids for giving me a reason to push beyond myself. Without them, I'd just be sitting around reading everyone else's books.

About the Author

Katie Lee O'Guinn has lived in many places but enjoys living in the Rocky Mountains now with her children. For more information on Katie Lee's books, check out www.katieleeoguinn.blogspot.com . She has two favorite quotes: "The Creative Adult is the Child Who Survived" and "We must always take sides. Neutrality helps the oppressor, never the victim. Silence encourages the tormentor, never the tormented." – Elie Wiesel

Katie Lee spends her time being a mother, a writer and volunteering for The Millstone Foundation, a foundation for the protection of children from Sexual Abuse, Sex Trafficking and Child Pornography. For more information on The Millstone Foundation, go to www.millstonefoundation.com.

18153304R00119